*Flight
from
Fifth
Avenue*

Also by Catherine M. Rae

Flight from Fifth Avenue

Catherine M. Rae

St. Martin's Press
New York

F
RAE

FLIGHT FROM FIFTH AVENUE.
Copyright © 1995 by Catherine M. Rae. All rights
reserved. Printed in the United States of America. No
part of this book may be used or reproduced in any
manner whatsoever without written permission except
in the case of brief quotations embodied in critical
articles or reviews. For information, address St. Martin's
Press, 175 Fifth Avenue, New York, N.Y. 10010.

Design by Junie Lee

Library of Congress Cataloging-in-Publication Data:
Rae, Catherine M.
    Flight from Fifth Avenue / Catherine M. Rae.
        p.   cm.
    ISBN 0-312-11788-4
    I. Title.
PS3568.A355F58   1995
813'.54—dc20   94-37517
                                                    CIP

First Edition: February 1995

10 9 8 7 6 5 4 3 2 1

For Lucy

Part One

chapter one

The Jardine mansion at the corner of Sixty-first Street and Fifth Avenue, in which I grew up, and from which I fled one cold, blustery night in February 1911, is to be demolished in order to make room for a twelve-story apartment house. I read that in the *Times* this morning. In the photograph accompanying the article, one taken around the turn of the century, I can just make out the tradesmen's entrance on the Sixty-first Street side, through which I made my escape. To this day a shudder runs through me when I recall the horror of the scene I had left behind me, and the terror I felt at the thought of being caught and brought back to a life that threatened to become intolerable.

I have no need of the photograph to remind me of either the austere, gray exterior of the house or the disposition of the luxuriously furnished interior. When we were little, my cousin Estelle and I played a game that involved assigning a certain smell or scent to the various rooms, and even now, fifty years later, whenever I detect a slight whiff of lemon furniture polish, I am momentarily transported back to the large front hall, where the Duncan Phyfe table and its two side chairs gleamed from the daily ministrations of the housemaids. The formal reception room to the left of the entry and the green-and-gold drawing room beyond it conjured up the heavier scents of the flowers that were replaced each day. To the right of the front door was the morning room, which I always associated with the peculiar smell of the yard-goods counter in Lord & Taylor's—probably because one chair or another was reupholstered frequently. Right behind it, the dining room smelled better, like something rich, port wine or fruit cake.

Then came the kitchen, in which I spent as many hours as I could with Mrs. Groome, the cook, and Mollie, the kitchen maid. The smells there were naturally ever-changing, depending on what was in the oven or on top of the huge black stove. I remember running down the back stairs at the first whiff of apple pudding or gingerbread, confident of being allowed to sample whichever it was. Years later Mollie told me that Cook purposely left the door to the back stairs open at times so that I'd be sure to appear. Those two women were extraordinarily kind to me—they must have known how lonely I often was—and unless a formal dinner was in preparation, I was allowed to spread out my paper dolls or coloring books on one end of the wooden table in the middle of the room. I wish they'd taught me something about cooking, though.

The somewhat forbidding attitude of Collins, the butler, discouraged visits to his pantry, but once in a while, when he was in another part of the house, Estelle and I would push open the swinging door and glance around his tidy preserve. It smelled like silver polish. We weren't particularly interested in that, but we did love to sneak past the pantry door and into the conservatory at the rear of the house and to breathe in the warm, damp air redolent with the fragrance of mimosa, lilies, and damask roses.

The "catch-all" room, as Mother called it—today I suppose it would be known as a family room—was not only the most cheerful room on the first floor, but also the most comfortably furnished. There one could sink into the softness of the old chintz-covered sofa or one of the upholstered armchairs with a sigh, and without fear of being told to sit up straight. It was in this room that I was allowed to entertain girls my own age with hot chocolate and little cakes while their mothers sipped tea in the drawing room, and it was there that my cousin Estelle, Aunt Eulalia Morrison's daughter, passed on to me in whispers what she had learned about marriage from one of the maids in the Morrison household.

"It's supposed to be fun," she said with a frown, "but I don't see how . . ."

"Why did Olga tell you all this?" I asked, not a little puzzled.

"Oh, I caught her kissing a picture of a man, and asked her why she was doing it." Estelle was just as much of a snoop as I was when we were eleven or twelve years old.

"I'm not sure I believe it," I said. "I can't picture Mother—"

"Of course you can't," she said sharply. "She's too old now. That all happens when you're first married. Look, Maida, don't go asking her about it. It will only get us into trouble. After all, you and I are only eleven and a half, and we're not supposed to know these things. Let's talk about something else—did you get a new dress for Caroline Colbert's birthday party? Oh, and do you think Mrs. Groome will let us have another piece of cake?"

It was in that same room that my brother Jerome taught me to play cribbage one rainy afternoon after listening to my troubles.

"Tell me who's been mean to you, Maida honey," he said after a quick glance at my tear-stained face, "and I'll beat him up."

"You wouldn't beat Mother up, would you? She's kept me

in the house for over a week—Henry says it's bronchitis, but I don't think bronchitis could possibly last that long—and made me miss the Thanksgiving play at school. And I was supposed to be Priscilla! All the girls wanted to be Priscilla, and I was picked, and now . . ."

"There'll be other plays, you know. Maybe you'll be picked for Juliet—"

"And not only that," I interrupted. "She's making me stay indoors for another whole week because I poured that awful liver tonic down the sink. I think Henry purposely ordered something that tastes horrible."

"I don't blame you, honey," he said with a little laugh. "I did the same thing once. The liver tonic and the raw-beef juice they thought I ought to drink went down the drain together. I had to write 'I will take my medicine' five hundred times. Look, find the cribbage board in that cupboard, and I'll teach you how to play. That will take your mind off things."

"Will you at least speak to Mother, Jerome, about next week? She always does what you want, and I can't stand another week in this house."

He nodded, and we settled down in front of the fire for my lesson. Piney, that's what the catch-all room smelled like, probably because of the wood we were burning.

The library on the second floor, with its massive leather furniture and shelves of expensively bound volumes, never quite lost the odor of Father's cigars, no matter how often Mother ordered the room cleaned and aired. On the evenings when they weren't going out or entertaining at home, he could be found up there, either reading in one of the big armchairs or bringing his journal up-to-date at the desk under the window. And he never chased me out, or told me to run along when I curled up with a book on the other side of the room.

Down the hall from the library, in the two upstairs sitting rooms, the scent of the potpourris of rose petals was faint and rather pleasant, while in the bedrooms, at least in those of my two sisters, one never knew what to expect. The unguents, salves, powders, and perfumes they used changed every time they went shopping (a frequent occurrence), sometimes for the good, and sometimes not. Alicia used to laugh when I made a face and held my nose, but Lenore would become angry.

"Maida!" she would cry out. "You are a consummate nuisance! You have no more manners than a street urchin! Mother shall hear about this." And the more I laughed, the shriller her voice became. She wasn't as pretty or as good-tempered as Alicia, but of the two she made the more brilliant marriage.

I seldom went into my parents' bedrooms or dressing rooms unless they were away on a visit or a trip, and when I did sneak in there, I never stayed long. I was too afraid that Collins or Lisette, Mother's maid, would see me and tattle. Father wouldn't have minded, I'm sure, but Mother would have scolded and lectured for half an hour. Her room always smelled delightfully of the French sachets she tucked behind the pillows on her chaise longue, while Father's men's cologne and tobacco permeated his.

My three brothers, Henry, Peter, and Jerome, had their quarters on the third floor. There was no sitting room up there, just their bedrooms, a small study, and the old schoolroom, which smelled of pencils, and was always somewhat dusty from the chalk my governess insisted on using when arithmetic was the subject. The only time I enjoyed being in that schoolroom was when Miss Crippleby, the seamstress, came to alter one of my sisters' dresses. If she had time, she'd help me cut out doll clothes, and when I was old enough she showed me how to stitch them up on the old Singer sewing machine in the corner.

Later on I had a German governess, my dear Fräulein Helff, who disliked the schoolroom as much as I did and managed to persuade Mother to let me have my lessons in the library. She was an utterly charming person, my Fräulein, and made the study of German a fascinating game for me. She rarely spoke a

7

word of English to me—only when I made a faulty translation in one of the Lieder or Geschichte she assigned. I loved her, and I loved the wonderful literature to which she introduced me, and when at the end of three years she left us to return to Germany, I was heartbroken.

"You mustn't cry, Liebchen," she said that last day. "You will always have me with you in spirit. And I am so proud of your progress; you would be at the top of your class at the Gymnasium at Bonn."

Life was not the same without her, but of course the rooms in the house were no different. Henry caught me snooping in his one afternoon when I thought they were all out, and he flew into such a rage that I didn't dare go up to the third floor for some time. I think it smelled of shaving soap.

The servants, of course, slept in the attics under the mansard roof, and the door at the bottom of the stairs leading up to their rooms was kept locked. Perhaps it's just as well that it was; with the exception of Mollie and Mrs. Groome, I don't think the help liked me very much, and if I'd been caught prowling among their possessions, I don't know what would have happened.

I suppose we could have managed quite well in a smaller house by putting the three girls in one bedroom, the boys in another, and my parents in a third, but the very thought of such an arrangement would have caused my mother to swoon and send people scurrying for the smelling salts. She had been born to wealth, had inherited wealth, and didn't know the meaning of the word "economize." Her only complaint about our spacious Fifth Avenue mansion was that we filled it up to the point where there were no proper guest rooms. I remember how jubilant she was when two of my brothers married and set up their own households. "At last, at last I shall be able to put people up overnight without embarrassment!" she exclaimed as she set about refurnishing the bedrooms.

In 1901 my brother Henry finished his medical studies and married Grace Garfield, whose father gave them a house on Madison Avenue for a wedding present. Mr. Garfield had made millions in the shipping business, and Mother quite approved of him and of the match, but when Peter married Ada Anne Alcott the following year, she was not at all pleased.

"What can Peter be thinking of?" she asked. "Who is she? No one ever heard of her, at least no one in society. What on earth has come over Peter? Doesn't he realize that it will be difficult for people to receive her?"

"He fell in love, Mother," Jerome said quietly. "He doesn't care about being 'received.'" And Peter didn't care. He concentrated on building up his brokerage business, and his life with Ada Anne and their children in a modest house on Forty-seventh Street. Jerome, the youngest of the boys, stayed home until 1905, when Great-Aunt Esther Jardine died. He'd always been a favorite of hers, but we had no idea of the depth of her affection for him until her will was read and we learned that she had left him the greater part of her not inconsiderable wealth. I doubt that Jerome ever did a full day's work after that, although he made a point of spending a few hours each morning at his office with Boyd and Fleming, stockbrokers.

Handsome, rich, and very much the charmer, Jerome was in constant demand among the society hostesses, especially those with marriageable daughters. He scarcely ever had a free evening, and when he did, it was used to rest up. Mother adored him, and had high hopes for his future, but whenever she mentioned marriage to him, he would smile and say, "I haven't found anyone who can compare with you, Mother."

While she reveled in that kind of flattery from him, she was not to be distracted from her determination to see him established in a Fifth Avenue mansion with a socially prominent wife.

"Jerome dear," she said one afternoon when he dropped in for tea, "old time is a-flying, you know, and you are not getting any younger. At twenty-six you should be giving the matter of marriage serious thought."

"You'll be the first to know, Mother," he answered, as he raised her soft white hand to his lips. "Besides, you are far too busy getting Alicia married to bother about me."

Mother was not only busy with plans for my oldest sister's wedding, she was also deliriously happy about the match Alicia was making. Stanley Welkin, of the Tuxedo Park and Palm Beach Welkins, was said by some to be the catch of the season, and Alicia, with her blue-eyed, fairy-princess type of beauty, had caught him. Apparently he had everything that she (and my mother) wanted: money, position, a Fifth Avenue address, and a "cottage" in Newport. He wasn't, however, much on looks, being a shade below average height and already showing signs of portliness.

When the wedding was over, Father took Mother to Paris to recover from all the excitement, and Lenore and I were left to ourselves in the big house. I was fourteen then, and she was three years older, but more than the difference in ages separated us. Like Mother, Lenore placed a high value on social position, and studied the society pages in the newspapers with the earnestness of a scholar preparing a thesis.

When our parents returned from Europe at the end of September, they were once more caught up in the social whirl, and Mother was hard at work launching Lenore into society. Father was the one who sensed that I was feeling left out (as a matter of fact, I'd been feeling that way for most of my life), and insisted that I be allowed to come to the dining room for meals when there were no guests. Mother protested that the other children had had to wait until they were fifteen to come to the table, but he gently and firmly overruled her. I still had many a lonely dinner in the morning room, since they entertained or were entertained several nights a week, but I was grateful to Father—particularly grateful when I realized he was making a special effort to include me in the conversation when the four of us did dine alone.

It didn't take Lenore long to get what she wanted, and by the time she was nineteen, her future was ensured. I don't know how she managed it; she was too sallow and sharp-featured to be considered a beauty (although she did have gorgeous red-gold hair), so it must have been her persistence—and, of course, her dowry—a word that made Father grimace every time it was uttered. In any case, on a beautiful day in May, Lenore married the oldest son of the Marquess of Scale, and went off to live in northern England. Mother was ecstatic and rarely lost an opportunity to refer to "my daughter, Lady Scale, you know." She also began to pay more attention to me, supervising my wardrobe, seeing that I had the best instruction in French, dancing, and music (this last was a complete waste of time, since I am tone-deaf), and taking me with her on occasion when she drove out in the afternoon to leave her calling cards at various great houses.

"Watch out, little sister," Jerome said with a smile one night after a dinner at which he had heard Mother criticize my posture and pronunciation in loud whispers. "She's grooming you for something. I wouldn't be surprised if she tried to snag a duke or a prince for you in a few years. She has titles on her mind, and you're not a bad-looking kid."

"I'll run away," I said, watching Collins hand around the tiny gold-and-white cups of after-dinner coffee. "I'll certainly run away rather than marry a scarecrow like the heir to Scale."

"And where would you run to?" he asked in the tone one would use to a fractious child.

"Into the wilderness, and I'd live with the Indians," I answered. I'd been reading James Fenimore Cooper, and discussing Magua with Father. "Some of them are quite handsome, judging from the pictures I've seen."

Before he could comment on that statement, Mother signaled to him to come and sit by her, and I was left to wonder whether he'd been serious in his warning or merely making light conversation, something Jerome was very good at. Beyond that, though, Jerome always made me feel that he was interested in me as a person, which none of my other siblings had ever bothered to do.

When I caught his eye and smiled across the room at him, he went right on talking to Mother, but he winked broadly at me when she leaned over to place her cup on the marble-topped table in front of her.

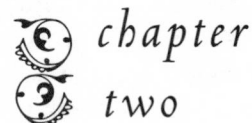

chapter two

I am not sure just what Jerome meant by that mischievous wink, but I know definitely that from that time on a closer relationship developed between us. He had moved into a suite of rooms at his club after he inherited Great-Aunt Esther's money, but he was frequently at the Fifth Avenue house—mostly at Mother's request. Occasionally, though, he came when she was out, and then he and I would sit in the catch-all room and talk or, if the weather was good, we'd go for a walk in the park.

"Try to look more grown up, Maida," he said one afternoon as we strolled toward the zoo to watch the seals. "That woman we just passed thinks I'm robbing the cradle."

"If I were allowed to put my hair up I'd look older," I said, "but Mother—"

"Yes, I know," he interrupted, "but pretty soon you are going to have to stand up to her."

"Jerome!" I was shocked. "Do you want me to rebel? Do you want me to be punished?"

"Of course not, honey. I just want you to begin to think for yourself. It's time you stopped being so biddable."

"It's easy for you to talk like that, Jerome, but it's different for girls. I mean, the rules are different."

He nodded, and started to say something about how rules could be broken, but just then we arrived at the pool where the seals swam lazily around in the sunlit water, and he didn't finish whatever it was he had begun to say.

From various remarks dropped at family gatherings—occasions like holiday or birthday dinners—I knew that Henry, a successful surgeon, and Peter, a hardworking stockbroker, thought Jerome was frittering his life away. Probably Alicia and Stanley Welkin were of like mind, and heaven only knows what Lenore would have said had she been present. (I was glad she was on the other side of the ocean.) I never heard Father comment on his youngest son's way of life, and of course in Mother's eyes he would be absolutely perfect if he would only marry well.

At the time I, too, thought of his life as being rather lazy and somewhat selfish, but that in no way lessened my affection for him. Then, one cold December afternoon, I changed my mind. I was standing at the window watching the first flakes of snow drift slowly down onto the trees on the other side of the avenue when a cab drew up in front of the house. A moment later Jerome jumped out, and after turning to speak to the driver, he ran up the steps to the front door.

"Get your wraps, Maida," he called when he saw me hurrying down the stairs to meet him. "We're going to a Christmas party."

"I shall have to change—" I began.

"No, no, it's not a dressy affair. Just bundle up. It's starting to snow."

"Is that you, Jerome?" Mother called from the drawing room where she was waiting for Mr. Rellenbach, who was expected for tea that afternoon. "Come in here, dear. I haven't seen you for over a week. Stay and have tea; Richard Rellenbach will be here shortly."

I don't know what he said to Mother while I was putting on my warmest cloak and the fur-trimmed bonnet that tied under my chin, but I am quite sure he did not mention our destination. He'd always been good at evading a direct question.

"Do you know Mr. Rellenbach, Jerome?" I asked as we went down the steps. "Who is he, anyway? And why does he come to see Mother so often?"

"He is a *very* wealthy man, Maida, rich as Croesus. No one knows exactly how many banks and companies he controls. But whether he's trying to get at Father through Mother—to invest money in one of his businesses—I just don't know."

"Where is the party?" I asked once we were in the cab and heading up Fifth Avenue. "And is that a present for someone?"

"Yes, a toy for a little girl. Did you ever hear of the Foundling Hospital, Maida?"

"The orphanage? Yes, of course. Is that where the party is?"

He nodded, and a few minutes later we stopped in front of the old, rambling red brick building on Sixty-eighth Street and Lexington Avenue, where so many of the city's abandoned children were housed.

"This is my sister Maida," he said to the sweet-faced nun who greeted us at the door. "Maida, this is Sister Mary Veronica, a good friend of mine."

"And your brother is a *very* good friend of the Foundling Hospital," the nun said. "I am happy to meet you, Maida. Come this way; I'll show you where to put your cloak and hat, and then take you in to see the children. The Christmas tree was set up this morning, and the little ones are in a great state of excitement."

She led the way across the wide entrance hall with its imposing marble staircase and threw open the door to a large, high-ceilinged room. Twenty or so children were gathered around a giant spruce tree that was decorated with silver tinsel and brightly colored ornaments. The children, who seemed to me to range in age from three to five years, all wore pretty little dresses or suits, which surprised me. I had expected them to be in some sort of uniform, and said as much to Sister Mary Veronica.

"Oh, we do not lack for clothing, Maida," she said with a smile. "Wealthy families are very good about sending us things their children have outgrown. You'd be surprised at how generous people can be—your brother, for instance. He is responsible for that lovely tree and all the trimmings."

I glanced at Jerome, who was holding one of the smaller girls in his arms while a little boy tugged at his jacket with one hand and pointed to the tree with the other.

"They all love him," the nun said, following my gaze, "and vie for his attention every time he comes."

"Does he come often?" I asked.

"Oh, yes, at least twice a week, sometimes more frequently. See the little girl he's holding? That's Anne Marie. She was left in a basket on our doorstep with a note pinned to her blanket telling us her name. She's a darling child, bright and cheerful, but with a strong will of her own. For almost two weeks she refused to eat her cereal at supper, no matter how much sugar we put on it. We didn't know what in the world to do—our menus here are quite limited—and then one evening Mr. Jardine sat down with her. What he talked to her about I cannot say, but as we watched in amazement, she cleaned up her bowl. She calls him Mr. Dino, and whenever he comes she swarms all over him."

At that point a rotund, bewhiskered Santa Claus carrying a huge bag on his back made his entrance, and a hush fell over the room.

"It's Mr. Duffy, the janitor," the nun whispered. "He does

this every year, and his performance improves as time goes on. We've prepared the children for his appearance, with pictures and stories, you know, but some of the younger ones are bound to be timid at first about going up to him for their presents. It won't take long, though, for him to win them over."

I watched, fascinated, as the wide-eyed children slowly approached the stepladder on which Mr. Duffy perched, his bag of toys on the floor in front of him. He greeted each child by name as he handed out the presents: rag dolls for the girls, toy soldiers for the boys, and candy canes for everyone. When the bag was empty he had them all sit down on the floor in a circle while he stood in the center and recited "The Night Before Christmas," complete with gestures.

"Would you like to see Christina now, Mr. Jardine?" the nun asked Jerome when he came over to where we were sitting.

"I would very much like to, Sister," he replied. "Just let me pick up the package I left in the hall."

"Christina is in the infirmary," Sister Mary Veronica explained while we waited for him to come back. "She had such a severe throat infection that we were afraid we were going to lose her, but she's making a good recovery now."

The pretty little girl in a crib near a window was sitting up, turning over the pages of a cloth picture book and humming to herself. When she saw Jerome she let the book fall and put out her arms to be picked up. Her face fell when he said it was too soon for her to be out of bed, but brightened again when he opened the box he'd brought and took out three teddy bears.

"See, Christina, here we have the whole family: Papa Bear, Mama Bear, and Baby Bear, just like the ones in the storybook," he said, arranging the bears in a row against the railing of the crib and smiling down at the child.

Christina hugged each bear in turn before setting them in a row again, and when we turned to leave she was murmuring softly to them.

"She's probably telling them a story," the nun said. "She knows plenty of them, because she won't settle down for the night unless we tell her one."

"How did you come to know about the Foundling, Jerome?" I asked as we drove home through the swirling snow. "Did someone introduce you to Sister Mary Veronica?"

"Well, yes," he answered. "What happened was this: I'd been visiting some friends up on Seventy-ninth Street, and decided to walk home. It wasn't late, only about ten o'clock at night, when I saw a man put a basket down against the railing outside the Foundling Hospital. I suppose he had been going to carry it up to the doorway of the building, but when he saw me looking at him he took off as if the Furies were after him."

"What did you do?"

"As soon as I saw that there was a sleeping baby—a very tiny one—in the basket, I picked it up and rang the doorbell. The nun who answered the door thought I was the father of the child, and was trying to persuade me to keep it when Sister Mary Veronica came along. That's how it started . . ."

"Was the baby Christina?" I asked.

"No, it was a little boy. I started visiting him, and then I saw Christina." He paused for a moment and then turned and looked at me. "I want to adopt Christina, Maida," he said softly.

"Jerome! How—"

"Yes, *how* is the question. I must marry first, and provide her with a mother. Another question is who? I thought becoming a Catholic would be the hard part, and it did take time, but it's been a wonderful experience. I'm still taking instruction—"

"Why are you becoming a Catholic?" I was astonished, and not for the first time that day.

"You see, since she was found in Saint Vincent Ferrer's Church, the assumption is that her mother was a Catholic, and therefore Christina must go to a Catholic family."

"Do Mother and Father know?"

"Of course not. Oh, they'll find out in time, but it's my life, Maida."

"Why did you pick Christina to adopt, Jerome, instead of the little boy you rescued?" I asked after a moment or two.

He turned his face away from me and looked out at the snow-covered avenue before answering. "I chose her," he said slowly, "because she reminds me of someone."

If the trip home had been a longer one—it isn't very far from Lexington and Sixty-eighth to Fifth and Sixty-first—Jerome might have told me about his lost love, but then again he might not. In any case, I had no chance to pursue the subject in the cab, and as soon as we arrived home Mother, who had been supervising the trimming of the drawing-room tree, took charge of my brother.

"Oh, Jerome, you are just in time!" she exclaimed. "Neither Collins nor I can get these last few angels to stand up properly. You may go now, Collins; Mr. Jerome will take over. Maida, go upstairs and change for dinner; wear your moiré skirt and a long-sleeved silk blouse. It is no night for bare shoulders; I've been feeling chilly all day."

Knowing that she would be annoyed at any interruption to her tête-à-tête with her favorite, I stayed upstairs until the gong sounded for dinner, thinking over the astonishing events of the day. I opened the curtains in my room and stared out into the darkness, recalling the scenes at the Foundling Hospital, the tiny babies in their cribs, the older children around the tree, little Christina hugging her bears, and Jerome holding Anne Marie. I'd seen a side of my brother's character unsuspected by the rest of the family, and a far cry from the "man-about-town" attitude he affected. That's the way he was at dinner that night, teasing Mother gently about the price she'd paid for the Tiffany angels and, more seriously, asking Father's opinion concerning certain investments he was considering. I wondered what he would say if Mother asked him where he had taken me that afternoon, but she was too intent on trying to persuade him to go with Father and her to the Goulets's ball the following night to take any interest in my activities.

"I doubt that I'll be able to make it, Mother," Jerome said carefully. "I have a dinner engagement—"

"But the ball does not start until ten o'clock, dear," she protested. "Surely—"

"Well, I'll try to make it, Mother," he said reluctantly. "I'll put in an appearance if it is at all possible."

"Yes, do, darling," she said, rising from the table. "And now, if you will excuse me, I think I'll make it an early night. It's been a tiring day, and I want to be rested for tomorrow. Come, Maida."

"She doesn't look well; she's been doing too much," I heard Father say softly to Jerome as I followed her out of the room, leaving the men to their port.

At the foot of the stairs Mother paused and put her hand up to her forehead as she leaned against the newel.

"Let me take your arm going up, Maida. I am really quite worn out. I can't imagine why." She was almost whispering, as if speaking in her normal voice would entail too much effort. She leaned heavily on my arm as we mounted the stairs, pausing from time to time so that she could catch her breath. Once in her own room, she sank down on the chaise longue and closed her eyes.

"Mother, what is it? Shall I—"

"Yes," she said hoarsely, "call Lisette. She'll help me to

bed. I'm just terribly tired—and cold. But I'll be fine in the morning, after a night's rest. Oh, I have so much to do tomorrow—the final fitting of the new gown . . ."

I rang for her maid, and waited until the devoted French-woman came and took charge. Lisette had been Mother's personal maid ever since I could remember, and could be trusted, I knew, to make her comfortable for the night. I closed the door quietly and hurried back down the stairs, hoping to have a chance to talk to Jerome, but he had left as soon as the men finished their port. I suppose he'd had enough of me for one day.

"Your mother isn't at all well, Maida," Father said when I went down to breakfast the next morning. "I have sent for Henry; he will know what to do."

"Should I go up and see if there's anything—"

"No, no. She said she wanted to be alone, but I told Lisette to stay in the anteroom in case she calls. I don't like it, Maida. I don't like it at all. What the devil can be keeping your brother? I phoned over an hour ago. Ah, there's the doorbell! Show Mr. Henry in here, Collins."

Henry listened patiently while Father described how Mother had been overdoing it lately and questioned me closely concerning the trip upstairs.

"You are sure she was short of breath, Maida? Yes? And complained about feeling cold?"

"Yes, terribly tired and cold, Henry. But she said she'd be all right after a night's rest, so I thought—"

"Yes, of course. I'll go up and have a look at her now—no, stay here, Father. It's better that I see her alone."

"It's serious, very serious," Henry said when he came down to the morning room after examining Mother. "Possibly pneumonia, and I suspect anemia. I've called Dr. Colson, a lung specialist, and Dr. Wilfred Ames. They'll be here shortly. She'll need careful nursing, day and night. Do you want me to arrange for it?"

Father merely nodded and turned away from us to stare out the window. "Stay with him, Maida," Henry said softly. "I'll get back to Mother. When Colson and Ames come, send them up at once."

From that moment on I think we all spoke softly, almost in whispers, and an unnatural quiet settled over the household. Bells on doors and telephones were muffled (quite unnecessarily, I thought, since Mother's room was protected by two heavy doors, one to the little anteroom to her bedroom, and one to the room itself), and what little conversation there was we carried on in hushed voices.

Father went to his office at the bank for a few hours every morning, and for the rest of the day secluded himself in the second-floor library, to be close at hand, he said. He didn't just sit there and brood, though; whenever I looked in on him, he was either reading or writing in his journal, or else going over the household accounts.

"I do not wish to see anyone, Maida," he said. "Will you be good enough to deal with any callers? Oh, and you'd better go through your Mother's engagement calendar and cancel everything for the next month."

He didn't seem unhappy or unduly worried about Mother, just slightly concerned about her comfort, and I wondered one evening when I saw him settling down after dinner with the late paper if he wasn't somewhat relieved that the round of pre-Christmas parties had been canceled.

Christmas Day itself was anything but merry. I remember that the carefully trimmed trees, the piles of presents, the pots of poinsettias, and the holly branches looked sadly out of place that year. At one point my sister Alicia suggested that it all be cleared away, but Father wouldn't hear of it; the noise and confusion might disturb Mother.

"At least we could open the presents," she persisted. "That wouldn't make any noise."

There were eight of us in the drawing room that evening— Henry's wife, Grace, Jerome, Peter and his wife, Ada Anne, Father, Alicia, Stanley, and I, waiting for Henry to come down and report on Mother's condition. Alicia looked expectantly from one to the other of us, but just then Henry came in, and no one paid any attention to her. There was no perceptible change, he said, but Mother seemed to be holding her own.

Father nodded, and after a perfunctory "Good night," left the drawing room. I remember that as we watched him go, Peter shook his head and said that it was too bad that his last Christmas here had to be such a sad one. Early in January he and his family were moving to Raleigh, North Carolina. One of Ada Anne's uncles had offered him a partnership in his brokerage firm there.

A few minutes later they were all gone, but not before Alicia had packed up the presents marked with her name to take home with her. She was, I thought, in spite of her wealth (or maybe because of it) overly fond of possessions.

I remember only two of the presents I received that year: a set of opals, necklace, bracelet and earrings, from my parents, and the ugliest handbag in the world from Aunt Eulalia. It looked more like a travel bag than anything else, with its metal corners and black leather covering. I couldn't imagine why she gave me such a thing, and later on when I showed it to Mother, she laughed.

"Just like Eulalia," she said. "She never had any taste. She probably bought it in Europe, thinking she could get better workmanship there. Oh, put it away for now, and after a while give it to one of the maids."

The week between Christmas and New Year's seemed endless, but when on the second of January the doctors announced that Mother was out of danger and on the road to recovery, I felt as if a fresh breeze had suddenly been wafted through the house. She seemed somewhat languid the first time I was allowed to see her, but that, I was told, was to be expected after such a severe attack of pneumonia.

By the middle of the month she was permitted to be out of bed, and it was then, I believe, that I noticed the first, almost imperceptible, change in her behavior. Before her illness she had presented to her family as well as to the outside world an open, calm countenance, one that remained unruffled and clear-eyed even when she was displeased. Now, though, I noticed a sly, calculating expression at times, and once in a while a strange smile that I can only describe as crafty—or maybe secretive. When she began to issue contradictory orders to the distracted maids, and I saw how worried Father looked, I way-laid Henry on his way out one evening and asked him about her condition.

"No, Maida," he said, pulling on his gloves, "her mind isn't going. She's merely reacting to the strain of her illness. You see, she's always been in such good health, and this, in a way, is her rebellion against not feeling top-notch. You'll see, she'll snap out of it."

I wanted to believe him, but when she dumped her breakfast tray on the floor the next morning and screamed that the toast was cold, I wondered. I could only hope that when she was fully recovered she'd revert to her old self. She did seem somewhat better after the nurses were dismissed and the household returned to normal.

"Oh, those nurses!" Mrs. Groome said to me. "I'm so glad they're gone! All those trays—and at all hours. That night nurse wanting her dinner at midnight, and hot, mind you! And then her breakfast at six in the morning!"

It hadn't been an easy time for any of us, and by the end of January I felt as if I had been cooped up in the house for months. I was restless, bored and, worst of all, feeling completely useless, no longer needed, since Mother was well enough to receive callers in her upstairs sitting room, and Father had returned to his usual activities.

I was lonely, too. My two best friends, Marjorie Ainsworth and Paula Harris, were both abroad at a school in Lausanne, learning to speak French, and my cousin Estelle was in Atlantic City with her parents. I didn't like Brenda Billingsly well enough to ask her to come to tea, but I think if she had invited me to her house I would have gone, just for something to do.

When the phone rang one bright, sunny afternoon, I hoped desperately it was Jerome, saying he wanted to go for a walk in the park, but the call was for Mother. I moped about for a few minutes and then hurriedly put on my coat and hat and told Collins I was going shopping. He looked surprised, probably because it was not customary for me to go out alone, but after all, my seventeenth birthday was only a week away.

I walked over to Bloomingdale's store on Lexington Avenue and took my time picking out two pairs of hand-sewn French kid gloves, the kind my sisters wore, not the plain ones I'd always had. I was wondering what else to buy when I noticed a display of dolls on a nearby counter, and a picture of Christina hugging her bears flashed across my mind. A short time later I was on my way to the Foundling Hospital with a soft, cuddly baby doll in my arms.

"She loved the doll," Sister Mary Veronica said when she opened the door for me the following afternoon. "She calls it her Maida doll. I'm sorry she was having her nap when you came yesterday, but she's awake now. Would you like to see her?"

That's how it began; from then on, whenever I could manage to make some excuse to go out, I visited the old red brick building and spent two or three hours playing with the children and helping the nurses in any way that I could. At first I simply amused the little ones in the day nursery by reading to them, telling them stories, or drawing pictures for them, but after a while Sister Mary Vee, as she had told me to call her, asked me if I would like to learn how to bathe and feed the infants.

"That's where we're so short of help, Maida," she said with a sigh. "Do you think—"

"Oh, Sister, I'd love to help, but I'd be afraid—"

"Because they're so tiny?" she asked with a smile. "You needn't worry, child. They're tougher than they look. Come, I'll have Sister Agnes show you what to do. She's almost at her wits' end."

"But Christina—she'll miss me."

"You'll have time for her, too, my dear, but you'll do more good in the infants' room."

Sister Agnes, a short, cheerful nun seldom seen without a baby in her arms, greeted me warmly, and before I could tell her that I knew nothing about infants, she had me settled in a rocking chair with a bottle in my hand and a screaming baby on my lap.

"He's hungry, dearie," she said, laughing at my bewildered expression. "Here, hold his head up a bit, so that the milk goes down easily. That's it. You're doing fine. When the bottle's empty, put him on your shoulder and pat his back like this, and after he burps lay him down on his side in that crib over there."

I was terrified that first day of doing something wrong, of dropping a baby or worse, but in a short time I was carrying them around confidently, feeding them, changing them, and bathing them as if I had always known how it was done.

I was giving Robbie Burns, a little black boy, his bath one afternoon, carefully washing the folds of his short neck with a soft cloth, when I became conscious of someone standing behind me.

"This is Maida, Doctor," I heard Sister Agnes say. "A natural if I ever saw one, bless her heart. Dearie, this is Dr. Risley, come to check on the formulas."

"I had better not shake hands with you right now, Dr. Risley," I said, "but I am happy to meet you."

"We'll shake hands another time, Miss Maida," he said, smiling down at me. "I am delighted to make your acquaintance, and it looks as if Robbie is as well."

Sister Agnes called to him to look at a baby who had been fussy all afternoon, and with another smile and a wave, he turned away. He looks too young to be a doctor, I thought as I walked home in the dusk. He has dark hair and is so tall and slender, not like the heavy, gray-haired men who came to take care of Mother. Even Henry is beginning to go gray, and he never seems to smile. I think maybe Dr. Risley reminds me of Jerome . . .

I hadn't seen very much of Jerome since New Year's Day; he had visited Mother, of course, but instead of staying to chat with me afterward he'd hurried away, saying he was unusually busy just then. I didn't see him that day, either, but about a week later he caught up with me as I was leaving the hospital.

"Maida! Why didn't you tell me what you were up to? This is wonderful!" he exclaimed, giving me a hug. "What does Mother say?"

"Nothing, Jerome, because she doesn't know. She's so concerned with her health and so busy planning—"

"Where does she think you go every day?"

"Well, it's not every day, and I don't think she cares what I do as long as I don't trouble her."

"That may be, but I happen to know something she has planned for you: Father is taking her to Palm Beach for a month, and you are expected to go along."

"Oh, no! I hate Palm Beach! I won't go!"

"But Maida—"

"Jerome, you are the one who told me to begin to think for myself, and that's what I have been doing."

He laughed. "I can see that, honey, and you'd better start thinking up a good reason for staying home. Why do you dislike Palm Beach so much? It isn't so bad."

"I'm not sure, but I know I don't want to go. I want to stay here and help with the babies. They need me."

"I'm sure they do. Well, maybe we can think of something."

I was glad Jerome came into the house with me that evening, although in the end he didn't help matters much.

"Mrs. Jardine will see you in the drawing room, Miss Maida," Collins said in his usual dry voice when he let us in. "She is expecting you."

I glanced at Jerome, but he just patted my shoulder reassuringly before we entered the softly lighted room where Mother sat in her favorite brocaded chair.

"Sit down, Maida," she said abruptly. "I wish to speak to you."

She ignored Jerome, which was quite unlike her, and watched me while I moved over to the settee opposite her. I glanced at Father, who did not meet my eye, and waited.

"Alicia tells me you have been spending your afternoons in an orphan asylum. Is that true?" she asked quietly.

"The Foundling Hospital, yes."

"No matter what it is called," she said with an impatient shake of her head, "it is an orphan asylum. Maida, how could you? A young girl, gently brought up—"

"It's my fault, Mother," Jerome broke in. "I took her to a Christmas party there. The Foundling is one of my charities."

"That is a different matter, Jerome. You are a grown man, and may do as you please. But Maida is a young, inexperienced girl. There is a world of difference."

"How did Alicia find out?" I asked timidly.

"Her friend, Mrs. Warrington, saw you going in there when she had her chauffeur deliver some clothing. She, of course, waited in her limousine."

"They need help so badly, Mother. The babies—"

"That's enough, Maida. Think of all the diseases you could

be exposed to there! You may even have picked up those pneumonia germs in that place, and passed them on to me. I forbid you to go there ever again, do you understand me?"

Her voice had become shrill, sounding the way it did when she began to recover from her illness, and her eyes flashed angrily as she stared at me. A sudden silence fell in the room, and a moment or two later, when she was calmer, her voice was low and controlled.

"You will leave with us next week for Palm Beach, and when we return it will be time to prepare for the summer in Glen Cove. Then, in the fall, you will be presented to society. Now go and change for dinner. Jerome, you will dine with us tonight, will you not?"

I wanted desperately to appeal to Father for help, but when I stood up to leave the room and looked at him, his face was turned away from me. Later in the evening I caught him alone in the library and begged him to intercede for me. He listened thoughtfully to what I had to say, but in the end he merely said that I would have to comply with Mother's wishes.

"Peace at any price, is that it, Father?" I asked rudely.

He didn't answer me. I stood looking at him, thinking he looked as unhappy as I felt. Then I went to my room to write a letter to Sister Mary Veronica.

chapter four

"Here's a notebook to take with you, Maida," Jerome said the day before we left for Palm Beach. "Fill it with snide comments on how hard the idle rich work at amusing themselves. Who knows? You might even enjoy yourself."

"Don't encourage me to be any nastier than I feel, Jerome," I replied, tucking two volumes of Scott into a suitcase. "I have enough trouble being civil to Mother—she's so demanding that sometimes I think she's crazy. She hasn't left me alone for a minute since she heard about the Foundling. Oh, I can't stand it! How long will this go on?"

"Until you marry, honey. That's the way it is."

"Yes, until I marry someone she chooses for me. Well, I won't! I won't!"

"She generally gets her own way, you know, so watch out, Maida."

She did get her way with her plans for me for the next months: first Palm Beach (boring), then Glen Cove for the summer (not too bad), and finally my first "season" the following winter (trying). Everyone thought she was a marvel, and perhaps she was, for besides being a clever, charming hostess, she looked extremely lovely, even in her fifties. Her brilliant blue-green eyes (she often wore emeralds to complement them) and her beautifully coiffed auburn hair set off a flawless complexion which was never, as far as I know, exposed to the sun. She dressed expensively, of course, but conservatively, careful never to let the beauty of her clothes overshadow her natural charms.

She had lost considerable weight during her illness, so that her figure was as slender as in the picture of her as a young girl and later as a bride. Heads still turned when she entered a room. One evening at the Royal Poinciana Hotel I overheard a gentleman observe that Mrs. Jardine moved across a room like a queen. I felt like a waif as I trailed after her.

I had rather enjoyed the long ride south in the private railroad car that Mr. Bradley, a friend of Father's, had put at our disposal, but the monotony of our days at that ostentatious resort nearly drove me to distraction. Mornings were spent on the Breakers Beach, where ladies were forced to wear long black stockings with their bathing dresses (some of them also wore gloves that came up to their elbows). Father and I bathed, but Mother never went near the water, preferring to remain shielded from the sun under a large striped awning, where she sat with the same group of women morning after morning while keeping an eye on me. Was she, I wondered, afraid I'd run away, go live at the Foundling Hospital with Sister Mary Vee?

When I said to Father that she seemed quieter than usual these days, he replied that she was simply following the doctors' orders. "They warned her not to become excited or upset about anything, Maida; that's the reason she is not exerting herself as she used to do. She was very seriously ill, you know."

I nodded, but I could not dismiss the feeling that she was brooding, spinning a web, making plans, plans that involved me and my future. Since I never dared to bring up the subject with her, there was nothing I could do until she made a move.

It would all have been so different if she had only liked me better, or loved me the way she loved Jerome . . .

As I said, life at Palm Beach was monotonous: there was the daily excursion to the ocean; then, at one o'clock, we all went back to the hotel for the interminable eight-course lunch, after which we rested or went for little drives until tea time at the Poinciana's Coconut Grove. At seven forty-five we changed for dinner, another stupefying meal. Afterward we either took a stroll in the cool of the evening, or sat listening to a string ensemble in the music room. Finally, at eleven o'clock, we went wearily up to bed with nothing to look forward to except a repetition of the whole wretched performance the next day.

Aside from two giggly girls who kept to themselves, there were no young people at the hotel just then, only little children, who were generally kept out of sight by their nurses. I was an anomaly, and I was lonely. I wallowed in self-pity, hated Palm Beach with a vengeance, and relieved my feelings by writing in Jerome's little notebook with a pen dipped in vitriol after my parents had retired for the night. I was careful to return the notebook to him as soon as we returned to Fifth Avenue, for fear Mother would come across it.

"We won't have more than three weeks in New York," Mother said when we were settled in Mr. Bradley's private car for the trip home. "Can you arrange things at the bank so that we can leave for Glen Cove on the ninth of May, Julian?"

"Easily, my dear," Father answered affably, looking up from his paper. "No trouble at all. I believe that I shall go to the office only two or three times a week this summer."

"I should think twice a week would be sufficient," Mother said. "Go in on Tuesdays and Thursdays, so that you will be on hand when we have Friday-to-Monday guests."

"Yes, Eleanora, yes, of course, if that is what you prefer," he replied, holding the newspaper up so that I could not see his face.

"You will need some new summer things, Maida, and I do believe it is time for you to put your hair up. I shall make an appointment with Pierre for you. Sit up straight, for heaven's sake, child! You never see me slouching, do you?"

She busied herself with her lists and plans, Father dozed in his armchair, and I pretended to read my Waverley Novel while I tried to figure out a way to see Sister Mary Veronica before we left for the country. Marjorie Ainsworth ought to be back from Europe, I thought, and if she is, and I could go to her house for lunch or tea, I might be able to leave early, and then . . . No, better not to chance it just now.

chapter
five

The house in Glen Cove, a large, not unattractive country seat, was originally owned by a shipping magnate who, according to the story, liked to give enormous and frequent house parties. As a result, we had ten guest rooms, all of them fitted out with large four-poster beds. We would have had twelve of these rooms, but two had been converted into lovely, spacious bathrooms. The shipping magnate's guests of long ago had to make do with old-fashioned washstands in their rooms and the toilet at the end of the hall of the guest wing.

The family quarters in the central part of the house were more comfortable (to my mind at least) than the stiff formality of the Fifth Avenue house. The chintzes and cretonnes were brightly colored, the chairs and sofas invited one to relax, and even the so-called drawing room—really just a large living room—had a sort of used, or lived-in, look about it, something Mother would never have tolerated in the city. I cannot, however, remember any distinctive scents or smells in that house, possibly because we were outdoors so much, or maybe because the windows and doors were generally open.

The summer of 1910 differed from previous ones spent at

Glen Cove only in that I was expected to participate in the garden parties, tennis games, sailing expeditions, and whatever other diversions my mother arranged for her carefully selected guests, instead of being free to amuse myself. Occasionally her list included a young man, a relative of one of her acquaintances (with an eye out, I suppose, for a partner or escort for me during the coming season). For the most part, however, the visitors were middle-aged members of society, concerned only with the current gossip and *le dernier cri*.

My cousin Estelle, who stayed with us for the entire month of August while Aunt Eulalia and Uncle Norbert were abroad, was, in Mother's eyes, a definite asset to a party. She chatted amiably with the women, flirted mildly with the men, and entered into the various planned activities with enthusiasm.

"Mark my words," Mother said as we watched Estelle demonstrate a new dance step to the group gathered around the piano, "she'll be a tremendous success next winter in New York. You would do well to emulate her, Maida."

I was sure my mother was right, but I had to smile to myself and wonder what she would have said had she seen my cousin's wicked imitation of Mrs. Grantly entering the drawing room, or heard her mimicry of Mr. Hapworth's affected English accent.

"It's a good thing Mr. Hapworth will not be with us next weekend," Estelle said one afternoon when we were walking along the beach, "because your ma told me that a *real* Englishman will be with us then, a Lord Somebody or other. What's the matter, Maida? You've suddenly gone white!"

I didn't want to tell her I was afraid my mother would marry me off to the first titled gentleman she could find, so I pretended a sharp shell had worked its way inside my thin sandal.

"He's staying with the Howards, and since they are coming, he had to be included," Estelle went on as I refastened the strap on my shoe. "He'll probably be a dreadful snob."

He wasn't a snob, and he presented no danger to me. The Earl of Delcannon turned out to be a harmless old fellow in his sixties who liked nothing better than to walk in the flower garden and talk about the roses he grew in Hertfordshire. Or so I thought at the time.

"Your father and I will be in Newport next weekend for the boat races, Maida," my mother said the day after we returned to the city, "and I shall give you a list of things that need attention while we are gone. You are to have three fittings on Friday, and to see the hairdresser Saturday morning. Then, in the afternoon, I want you to check on the calling cards I ordered from Tiffany's. They promised them for the fourteenth. Now, for goodness' sakes, go and try on the gown that arrived yesterday, while I try to think of what else to add to this list. Oh, and send Lisette to me at once."

I only half listened to her; the prospect of three days without her constant supervision made me feel almost giddy for a few minutes. I'll do everything on her list, I thought when my head cleared, and then . . .

"Of course you must respect your mother's wishes, Maida, my dear," Sister Mary Veronica said firmly late on Saturday afternoon as we moved along the corridor to the infants' nursery. "And while it may seem hard, even unfair to you now, you must understand that she has her reasons—"

"Not very good ones," I interrupted.

"Perhaps not by your lights, but by hers they are good ones. Oh, there's Sister Agnes! She has missed you greatly, Maida."

"Oh, Maida, my love," the plump little nun cried, embracing me warmly. "You've come back to me! Look here—hasn't little Robbie grown? He'll be running all over the place before we know it. And look at Baby Joy, isn't she a little beauty?"

I picked Robbie up and held him close to me while Sister Mary Vee explained the situation to her. Her face fell, but only for a moment. "Sure, you'll be coming back to me someday, Maida girl. Now don't cry, dearie, mark my words, if you don't find a way, the Lord will. Oh, my, there's Andy boy calling for his supper."

She hurried off to attend to the screaming baby, and we went on to the older children's room. I stayed just long enough to admire the way Christina had arranged her dolls and bears on a chair in the corner, and to listen to her exclaim over the colored pencils Jerome and a lady had brought her.

"Blue is for sky," she said seriously, "and green is for trees. See?"

I nodded, and let her lead me to the adjoining playroom where five or six little ones were gathered around a young nun at the piano singing "Twinkle, twinkle, little star." When Christina joined them I slipped out, wondering who the "lady" was Jerome had brought to see her.

"I shouldn't have come," I said to Sister Mary Vee when I stopped in at her little office to say good-bye. "Now I'll miss the babies more than ever."

"You probably will for a while, my dear, but remember this: you are not going to be a seventeen-year-old girl forever. The time will come when you will be your own mistress." She kissed me lightly on the forehead and watched me hurry out onto Sixty-eighth Street just as the sun was setting. I was halfway to Lexington Avenue when I was startled by someone falling into step beside me.

"Oh, excuse me, Miss Maida," Dr. Risley said apologetically. "I didn't mean to take you by surprise. I saw you leaving, and wanted to ask when you'd be coming back to us—why, you're crying! I shouldn't have—"

"It's not you—not that—it's just—"

"Would you care to tell me about it? Perhaps I can help."

I saw Collins glance at the hall clock as he opened the door for me a few minutes before six (Mother must have told him to keep tabs on me), but all he said was that Mr. Jerome would be coming to dine at eight o'clock.

"That's fine, Collins," I said, delighted at the prospect of my brother's company. "Do you think Mrs. Groome could make that apple tart he likes so much?"

"She's planning on it, Miss Maida."

I went upstairs and dawdled over a warm scented bath as I reviewed the events of the afternoon, especially the conversation I'd had with Dr. Risley as we walked down Fifth Avenue. He'd been shocked at my mother's attitude toward the Foundling, but in the end he advised me to abide by what Sister Mary Vee had said.

"Perhaps after your season as a debutante, which I gather holds little attraction for you, your mother will relent," he said, taking my arm as we crossed one of the side streets.

"I doubt that," I answered, glancing up at him. "She'll keep a tight rein on me until she's married me off to someone with a title. My sister Lenore is Lady Scale, and my brother Jerome says Mother wants me to be a duchess."

"Well," Dr. Risley said with a little laugh, "if that happens, you'll be able to do what you like."

"I don't intend to let it happen," I said. "I'll run away first."

"If I were you, I wouldn't make any rash decisions at the moment. Just get through this year, and take it from there."

We talked a little about the Foundling—he was deeply committed to his work there—and then, just before he left me at the foot of our stoop, he surprised me by asking if he might call.

I waited until Collins had left us after serving coffee in the drawing room before telling Jerome about my afternoon.

"What did you say when Dr. Risley asked permission to call?" he asked with a smile. "I've met him—nice fellow."

"Of course I said yes, but what Mother will say I don't know."

"If you choose to see him, little sister, perhaps it would be better if you arranged to meet him someplace else. You could always say you were meeting me, you know. Now, let me tell you what I've been up to. You'll be surprised. Ready?"

I was very much surprised. In preparation for his plan to adopt Christina, he'd bought a house on Washington Square East, he'd been received into the Catholic Church, and he was engaged to be married to Maria Teresa Desta.

"You'll like her, Maida. She's true blue, absolutely beautiful, and she loves Christina. Also, she has no money aside from her salary as a nurse. Mother will have apoplexy, but I can't help that."

"Oh, Jerome! How wonderful! When can I meet her?"

"Tomorrow if you like. We're going to the noon Mass at Saint Patrick's Cathedral, and then to lunch at the Waldorf. Would you like to come along?"

"Yes, I'd love it. Oh, this is wonderful news! I am so happy for you, Jerome. Now I know why you never came down to Glen Cove this past summer."

"I was far too busy, Maida. Too busy being happy for the first time since . . ." He paused and stared across the room for a moment or two.

"Since when?" I asked finally.

"Well, I guess I can tell you now. Five years ago I fell in love, deeply in love. Laura was a lovely girl, compassionate, charming, warm, everything I wanted. Then something went wrong with her health, kidney trouble of some kind, and she died after a long illness. I thought I would never love another woman, that it would never happen to me again, and it didn't, until I met Maria."

"You never told anyone?"

"No, I wanted no interference from the family. Laura was not a society girl. And now I think it's just as well that I kept quiet about it. Mother—"

"Oh, of course. She would have wanted Laura's pedigree."

"She would have rejected her, Maida, just as she'll try to reject Maria. In that case, however, she'll have to reject me as well."

I went to bed happy that night, happy for Jerome, and happy at the thought of seeing Dr. Risley again. I never did hear from him, though, and it was some time before I learned the reason why.

I have rarely seen a handsomer couple than Jerome and Maria made at lunch the next day in the quiet elegance of the old Waldorf. I liked her from the start, and I could see that Jerome was pleased with my responses to her overtures of friendship, even though he could hardly take his eyes from her lovely, animated face. She was a true Italian beauty, with warm brown eyes and masses of dark hair that waved softly back from a face that Fra Angelico might have painted.

I cannot remember everything we talked about that day, but by the time the meal was over I knew that Maria Teresa was twenty-four years old, that she had worked as a nurse in St. Luke's Hospital for three years, and that she wasn't at all sure what her surname really was.

"It's a bit of a mystery, actually," she said with a chuckle. "My parents and grandparents and their parents before them worked on the d'Este estates in Italy. My father came to America sometime in the 1880s. He knew practically no English, and somehow or other his name went down on his immigration papers as Desta. We think he probably tried to tell the authorities he had worked for the d'Este family, but of course we're not sure. Either he liked Desta better than his given name—neither he nor my mother would ever say what it was—or else he thought he'd been rechristened on Ellis Island."

"Well, you'll have a new name soon, love," Jerome said, smiling across the table at her.

"And what will your father think of that?" I asked.

"I may never know," she replied. "When my mother died a

few years ago, he packed up and went back to Italy. My two brothers went with him. It worries me that I hear from them so seldom."

"Didn't your father want you to go with him?" I asked.

"Yes," she answered, "he did, but I was doing so well in nursing school that he decided I should finish the course, and then join them. I keep meaning to go see them, but somehow . . ."

"I'll take you there anytime you say, Maria," Jerome promised. "A honeymoon, perhaps?"

They wasted no time: early in November they sailed for several months in Europe after being married in the Church of St. Vincent Ferrer, the church in which Christina had been found. Will Eldredge, an old friend of my brother's, and I were the only witnesses.

A letter addressed to my mother and father in Jerome's strong, masculine hand arrived the next day, and was read in ominous silence.

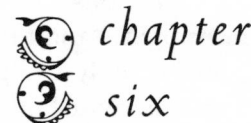 *chapter six*

More than once during the winter of 1910–11 I wondered if there wasn't something wrong with me. Why, instead of enjoying myself at the dinner parties, midnight suppers, and the balls that were *de rigueur* during the season, did I find myself waiting impatiently for the affair to be over so that I could leave? Oh, I went through all the appropriate motions; I put on an alert, interested expression when the young man on my right told me about his polo ponies, or the dullard on my left asked me for the third time if I didn't agree that Lillie Langtry was the greatest beauty of all time.

Perhaps I am not being fair; there were some enjoyable evenings, especially at the theater, and I did relish having my dance card filled almost as soon as I entered the ballroom. Also, I couldn't help being pleased when I was cited in the society column as "one of the most sought-after debutantes of the season." Mother, of course, was overjoyed.

"I never thought you had it in you, Maida," she said, giving the flounce of my pale-green satin ball gown a twitch as I waited in the drawing room for my escort to take me to the

Silvertons's pre-Christmas supper dance. "You are even more popular than Estelle. It's most surprising."

"She's a late-blooming rose, that's what she is," Father said, smiling across at me. "Nothing surprising about that."

"Well, she'd better make a match before the bloom wears off," Mother retorted. "It doesn't last indefinitely, you know, Julian."

"For God's sakes, Eleanora, she's not eighteen yet, and—"

"Old enough to start thinking about her future," Mother interrupted, "and I intend to see that she does."

Fortunately Collins announced Mr. Traherne at that moment, otherwise I might have lost my temper. As it was, I found it difficult to try to give the impression that there was nothing in the world I would rather do than attend the supper dance with him.

I was incredibly slow in realizing how deadly serious Mother was about marrying me off. I should have suspected that something was afoot when Lord Delcannon, he of the rose gardens in Hertfordshire, came to Mother's "Wednesday afternoons" three weeks in a row, and made a point of engaging me in lengthy conversations on each occasion. I thought at the time that he singled me out partly because he was unfamiliar with the other callers, and partly because, unlike some of the chatterboxes, I was a good listener. I may have wondered briefly why he came to dinner twice—no, three times—in January (Mother had never invited the same guest more than once a month), but actually I had no more interest in him than I would have had in one of Father's business acquaintances. I should have been more alert, more aware of the signals, but I wasn't, and in the end I was taken by surprise.

It all became clear to me one rainy afternoon early in February. I was in the upstairs sitting room that had been mine since my older sisters moved out, happy that there was no party or dance that night, and preparing to write a long letter to Jerome and Maria. I had just opened my desk when the parlormaid appeared in the doorway with a message.

"Excuse me, Miss Maida, but Mrs. Jardine asks that you dress for tea and come down to the drawing room as soon as possible," she said, glancing at the letter paper in my hand.

"Oh dear! Who is down there, Emma?"

"No one yet, miss, but Madam has ordered tea for four."

"Is my father there?"

"No, miss. So it must be two that are expected."

I hated tea gowns, but I knew Mother would be cross if I appeared in the striped silk I had had on all day. I chose the least elaborate dress in my wardrobe, a soft blue velvet with a wide sash, tidied my hair, and went slowly down the stairs. Lord Delcannon was standing in front of the marble fireplace, and next to him, lounging with one elbow on the mantel, was a tall stranger who was staring down into the flames.

"Ah! Maida, my dear," Lord Delcannon greeted me, taking my hand in both of his and looking as if he were about to kiss me. "I am delighted to see you. And you are looking so well! Allow me to present my son Edmund, Viscount Ormley, recently arrived on these shores."

The young man came forward and bowed politely, murmuring a few words I could not hear. I doubt that I even nodded in acknowledgment; I was too stunned by the sudden realization that this was the man chosen by my mother to be my husband. While he wasn't actually ugly, there was something repulsive, almost vulpine, about his looks. His face was narrow, his hair was red, and his small eyes were such a light brown that they looked almost yellow. I thought for a moment I was going to be sick.

"Maida, my dear." My mother's voice sounded artificial, and somewhat distant. "Maida, will you be so good as to pour? I think we are all ready for a hot cup of tea. It's such a dismal day."

I'll see it through, I thought, sitting down behind the silver tea service. I won't do anything to embarrass Mother, but if she thinks I'm going to marry that odious fellow . . .

The odious fellow took a chair near mine, and after asking for milk and two lumps, lapsed into silence. I, like a well-trained puppet, asked him how he was enjoying New York, whether he'd had a chance to go to the theater, et cetera, et cetera, to which he replied in monosyllables or merely with a shake of his head. At one point, when I turned from answering Lord Delcammon's inquiry about the best part of Central Park for a quiet walk, I caught Ormley's eyes on me. His expression was so cold and calculating that I quickly averted my glance and busied myself with the plates of sandwiches and dainties.

He does look like a fox, I thought, a fox getting ready to spring on its prey. Later, when the two men rose to take their leave, he bent his head slightly toward me and asked in a low voice if he might have permission to call on me in the near future. Before I could reply, Mother, who had incredibly keen hearing, cried out:

"But of course, my dear Viscount, you must call whenever it suits your pleasure."

I said nothing.

"What a splendid young man the viscount is, Julian," Mother said when the three of us sat down to dinner that night. "So very British! A viscount, and heir to vast estates! Didn't you admire him, Maida?"

"I'm afraid not," I said, making no effort to keep a note of distaste out of my voice. "I think he looks like a fox, and I know he'd been drinking. I could smell it on his breath when he sat next to me, and later on when he asked permission to call. Also, his hand was damp when he said good-bye."

"Oh, he probably had a glass of wine at lunch, just as your father often does," Mother said with an airy wave of her hand. "And as for a damp palm, he was feeling warm. He was, you will remember, sitting quite close to the fire. You are imagining things, Maida. Julian, I am thinking of having a dinner party . . ."

She said no more about the Delcannon heir until two days later when he called, at which time she was furious at me for sending down word that I was indisposed. I cannot possibly reproduce the long, angry lecture she read me on proper behavior after he left. Just let me say that she stood in front of me tight-lipped for a moment or two before scolding me in a low, controlled voice for a good quarter of an hour—a fine demonstration of "cold anger."

Not surprisingly, the viscount did not call again, but ten days later he appeared at my side at Estelle's birthday dance. I suppose Mother had told Aunt Eulalia to invite him.

"Miss Maida Jardine, if I am not mistaken," he said, raising his eyebrows slightly. "I trust you are recovered from your indisposition?"

"Yes, thank you, I am," I replied evenly. "I trust you are having a pleasant stay in New York?"

Before he could reply, Bobby Beaumont, a chubby young man without a brain in his head, claimed me for the waltz that was just beginning. From time to time during the rest of the evening, I was conscious of Ormley's yellow eyes on me, but he kept his distance until the party was over. He intercepted me as I went to fetch my evening wrap, putting his damp fingers on the bare part of my arm above my long white gloves. When I jerked away from him he laughed, and crossing his arms nonchalantly, said: "I shall call again, never fear."

"And I shall be indisposed again," I retorted.

He laughed once more, then turned abruptly away.

chapter seven

The dinner party that my mother had mentioned earlier took place on Valentine's Day. The sky had been a dull gray all afternoon, and by evening the first flakes of snow were drifting down past the glass of the conservatory where I went to find a camellia to pin to the bodice of my dress. I am not sure why I bothered. It wasn't to be what Father called a "state affair," but merely a family dinner. Alicia and Stanley would be coming, as well as Henry and his wife, Grace. Aunt Eulalia, Uncle Norbert, and Estelle had also been invited.

"A little festivity for Cupid's day," Mother had said at lunch. "A wonderful excuse for a mid-winter party. Wear your red watered silk tonight, Maida, and your opals. Yes, the opals, I think."

All unsuspecting (how trusting I was!), I did as she asked, and had just finished pinning the camellia to my dress when I heard the front door being opened. I hurried into the drawing room, prepared to greet Estelle and her parents—Aunt Eulalia always made a point of being the first to arrive at any party. I stopped suddenly on the threshold, though, so shocked at the sight of the group near the fireplace that I nearly grasped one of the portieres for support. Mother had her back to me, Lord Delcannon was helping himself to sherry from the tray Collins held, and his son was leaning carelessly against the mantel, just as he had been the first time I saw him. For an instant I thought wildly of running back upstairs, but before I could move, Mother turned and beckoned to me. It never occurred to me to ignore her summons, so conditioned was I to unquestioning obedience. I did, however, make a point of devoting myself to the senior Delcannon until the rest of the guests arrived.

Without Uncle Norbert's contributions, the dinner might have been a dreary affair. Henry, never a chatty person, had little to say, and Grace seemed to take her cue from him. Alicia, who had complained earlier of a headache, looked bored and disinterested. Lord Delcannon commented on the beauty of the bright-red roses in the centerpiece, but on little else, and Father, generally an excellent host, ignored Mother's signals to draw the Englishmen out, and concentrated on his plate.

The conversation was almost at a standstill when Uncle Norbert took charge. A natural and splendid raconteur, he could draw on a seemingly inexhaustible fund of anecdotes at a moment's notice, and come up with one appropriate to the occasion.

"This is an excellent saddle of lamb, Eleanora," he said, glancing at my mother. "I am reminded of a story about one that wasn't quite up to par. Admiral Entwistle, as crusty an old fellow as I ever saw, gave a dinner for some Navy brass one night. Now Entwistle, among his other pecularities—and he had many—liked to do his own carving, even though he had butlers and aides galore. This night, however, the carving didn't go very well. The admiral shouted that the meat was tough, and that he needed a sharper knife. The butler went out to the kitchen to find one, but before he returned, the cook, a temperamental fellow, rushed in and handed Entwistle a meat ax!"

"Surely, Norbert, you exaggerate," Aunt Eulalia protested amid the chuckle that ran around the table.

"He may, Eulalia," Father said, "but you must admit that he tells a lively story."

"That reminds me of the time . . ." and Uncle Norbert was off again. Viscount Ormley said little throughout the meal, nor did he so much as smile when the rest of us burst out laughing. He was seated directly opposite me, and each time I looked across at him he was either signaling Collins to refill his glass, or sitting motionless with his yellow eyes fixed on me. When Estelle, who sat on his right, asked him some question or other, he merely shook his head without looking at her.

"Watch out, Maida," she whispered as we followed the ladies into the drawing room, leaving the men to their port and cigars, "Delcannon *fils* has his eye on you."

"See if you can keep him occupied when they come in," I answered softly. "Or better still, sit next to me on the love seat; there won't be room for him there."

A good half hour passed before the men joined us, and then only Henry, Ormley, Stanley, and Uncle Norbert came in. Father and Lord Delcannon, Henry said, would be in shortly. They delayed so long in the dining room that when they finally did appear, the other guests were preparing to leave, and in the bustle of their departure I almost did not notice the abrupt change in Lord Delcannon's manner. He may have said good night to Mother, but he brushed past me without a word, and taking the slightly unsteady Ormley by the arm, hurried him from the room.

I thought that perhaps he was ashamed of his son's behavior, or that he suddenly felt unwell, but what I *hoped* was that something had happened that would make it impossible for either of them to call again.

I was half right. Later that night, when I tiptoed past Mother's room on my way to fetch a book from the library, I heard Father's usually pleasant voice raised angrily.

"It's an outrage, Eleanora! Two million dollars—"

"Julian, listen to me! You have embarrassed me dreadfully by refusing his offer. The money—"

"Aside from the money—Ormley is a fool!"

"You are mistaken. He is quiet and reserved; that is the nature of men in his position. And he probably feels a bit ill at ease in a foreign country, but he is certainly no fool." Mother's voice was so low, I could hardly hear her.

"And Maida?" Father was almost shouting. "Have you thought about her? Have you consulted her? She may—"

"Lower your voice, Julian. Maida will do as I say. I shall arrange things so that she will have to—"

"What things?"

"Never mind. And please do not forget that it is my money, left to me by my dear father, and I can do with it what I choose."

"No, you have never let me forget that, my dear. I have often wondered what our lives would have been like if you had been forced to live on what I provide—which, by the way, is no inconsiderable amount."

"Oh, for heaven's sakes! We've been over that dozens of times!" Mother exclaimed impatiently. "Now, listen to me: two million dollars is a reasonable dowry—"

"Have you taken leave of your senses? It's the most outrageous demand I have ever heard!"

"It *is* a reasonable dowry, a modest sum to pay to see a daughter become a viscountess, the wife of the heir to the earldom of Delcannon! Why, she'll be presented at court! And with Lenore as Lady Scale—"

"Maida is not Lenore," Father interrupted. "There is no comparison. I tell you, Eleanora, I will not consent—"

"Oh yes, you will, Julian. You know very well what a word from me could do to your reputation. Now, please go to bed. Leave everything to me; I'll smooth things over with Delcannon tomorrow."

At the sound of a chair being pushed back, I flew down the

carpeted hall to my own room, closed the door quietly, and stood leaning against it until my heart stopped pounding. I don't know which of the three items I'd overheard shocked me the most: that my mother meant me to marry Ormley no matter what; that it was she who held most of the family wealth; or that she knew something that could destroy Father's reputation. What could he have done?

I am not sure why I decided to say nothing until my mother brought up the subject of marriage. Possibly it was because I did not want her, or Father, to know I had been eavesdropping, or possibly because I thought that given time she might see how disastrous such a marriage would be. In any case, I said nothing.

She waited until the next evening, when Father was at a Republican League dinner, before mentioning Ormley.

"I have a wonderful piece of news for you, Maida," she said as we sat in the drawing room after dinner. "I've been saving it until you and I could have a quiet moment—"

"If you think—" I burst out.

"Please do not interrupt me, Maida. You know how rude that is. Now listen to me. You have been honored with a proposal of marriage from Edmund, Viscount Ormley, heir to the earldom of Delcannon! The marriage—"

"Will never take place!" I was shouting as I stood up. "Nothing will ever induce me to marry that man! How could you—"

"Sit down, Maida, and modulate your voice."

I neither sat down nor lowered my voice. I lost my temper completely. I accused her of subordinating any natural maternal instincts she might have to an overriding ambition. I accused her of greed, of treachery, and of selling her daughter into slavery. Had I been familiar with any obscenities then, I probably would have hurled them at her. In a word, I was beside myself, out of control. Finally, out of breath, I sank down on the sofa and wept.

I can almost smile now when I think of that scene, how like an excerpt from a cheap melodrama it must have looked, but I saw nothing to smile at then.

"Go up to your room, Maida. You are in no condition to listen to reason."

I dragged myself up from the sofa and had started for the door when it opened and Father came in. Before he could say anything, Mother took me firmly by the arm and led me to the foot of the stairs. I went up slowly, and when I reached the top I turned to look down at her. She was watching me, standing as still as a marble statue, and looking just as cold.

Reason told me that she couldn't have me carried bound and gagged to the altar, but that thought did nothing to lessen my terror. She was acting like a crazy woman. What would she do? Hadn't Jerome once said, "She generally gets her way"? Then I remembered that when I asked Father to persuade her to let me go to the Foundling Hospital he had answered that I would have to comply with her wishes. Was there no way out?

I took off my opal necklace and bracelet and brushed out my hair, but there was no point in going to bed. I knew I couldn't sleep, and after wrapping myself in the quilt that was at the foot of my bed I curled up on the window seat and looked out at the snow that was still falling lightly, wondering what on earth I could do.

I can't say I have a terrible disease, I thought. They'd call Henry, who would see through any pretense. And I won't kill myself, although if I knew how I might kill Edmund Ormley, viscount or no viscount—but then she'd just find another earl or duke. I'll have to go away, I thought, make good my old threat and run away. But where? Jerome was in Europe, Alicia and Henry would keep me under lock and key until Mother came for me. Maybe Peter . . . Maybe in the morning I'll think of something, I thought. I'm too tired now.

I undressed quickly and went to bed. I must have been sleeping lightly, for sometime later a sound in the hall caused me to sit up, clutching the bedclothes up to my chin. I switched on the lamp next to me just as Father appeared in the doorway with a finger to his lips and an envelope in his hand.

"You must go away, child," he whispered urgently. "Disappear. Hide someplace. Take a train to Canada—anyplace. It's the only way to stop this marriage. Take this money; it's all I have with me. Write to me care of the bank and I'll send you whatever funds you need."

I had never seen my usually calm, self-possessed father in such a state of anxiety. His hand was shaking, his voice was hoarse, and the look of desperation in his eyes frightened me. He was a man distraught.

"But where—" I began.

"No, no, don't talk!" he interrupted. "Just go. Don't use the front door; she might hear that. Go down the back stairs and out by the tradesmen's entrance. There's no hope for you here. Hurry, dress warmly and go!"

With that he left as quietly as he had come. For a moment I stared at the envelope he had thrust into my hands, unable to move until the sound of a door closing somewhere in the house startled me into action. I dressed quickly in the warmest clothes I could find in my hurry, a dark woolen skirt, a long-sleeved shirtwaist, a lamb's-wool sweater, and my red wool jacket with the French-braid trim. The only outer garment I had in my room was my velvet evening cloak, so I put that on, not daring to risk opening the coat closet downstairs. A suitcase of any kind was out of the question, since all of our luggage was kept in a special room on the third floor, so I stuffed the envelope and a few pieces of underwear into the ugly handbag Aunt Eulalia had given me one Christmas. It was the largest one I had.

A glance in the mirror showed me that I still wore the opal

earrings—in my hurry to get into bed I had forgotten to remove them—but I didn't want to delay any longer at that point. I went quickly to the rear of the hall and opened the door to the back stairs, praying that the hinges wouldn't squeak. The darkness of those stairs didn't worry me; as a child I had had to use them frequently, and I started down confidently. They still had the faint smells of polish and cooking that always lingered there—old friends, in a way.

I still didn't have any destination in mind; all I could think of was getting out of the house before someone stopped me. I almost didn't make it.

I pushed open the door at the bottom of the staircase while I was still on the last step of the stairs. The light near the stove that the cook left on in case anyone needed something during the night was dim, and at first I didn't see him.

Slowly, ever so slowly, a man rose from the old rocking chair in the corner where Mrs. Groome rested between chores. I retreated to the bottom step of the stairs as he approached me, and because of the poor light it was not until he had covered half the distance that separated us that I recognized Ormley.

"Surprised to see me, are you not, Miss Maida?" he asked.

When I made no reply he gave a short laugh before going on. "Your esteemed mother and I were having a nice little chat tonight, and when she realized the lateness of the hour as well as the inclemency of the weather, she invited me to stay the night. Always the perfect hostess."

"Get out!" I shouted. "Go away from—"

"Oh, no," he said with another short laugh. "And you are not going anyplace either. You see, my plan was to wait here, near those convenient back stairs, until you were well asleep, and then surprise you—no, compromise you—in your own little bed, but now that you are here . . ."

With that he moved quickly toward me, smiling horribly, ready to enfold me in his outstretched arms.

"No!" I cried, and in desperation swung the ugly leather

handbag at him with all my strength. The corner of the metal framework must have caught him on the side of the head, for I saw blood spurt out before he groaned and sank to the floor.

Appalled by what I had done, I moved closer to where he lay to assure myself that he was still breathing. Moments later I was out of the house and on the snowy sidewalk of Sixty-first Street, hurrying toward Madison Avenue, alone and afraid.

Sometime later, shivering with cold and exhaustion, I rang the night bell of the Foundling Hospital, feeling like an orphan myself.

chapter eight

Sister Mary Veronica acted swiftly. By the morning of February 17, I had been renamed Mary Wicklow and was on a train bound for Michigan in the capacity of supervisory agent for a group of homeless children.

"Much as we would like to have you here with us, Maida dear," she said the morning after my flight from home, "you cannot stay. Since your mother is aware of your association with us, she will be certain to look for you here. We have given the whole matter careful thought, and decided that since your father gave you permission, even urged you to go away, we are perfectly justified in helping you. Now, go upstairs to Sister Agnes while I make arrangements for your safety. Let me see— oh, yes—I must find a warm coat for you. That lovely velvet wrap will never do."

Two hours later she and I were in a cab on our way downtown, and during the trip she explained to me that the Children's Aid Society was in need of agents to accompany groups of orphans to various rural communities in the West, where homes would be found for them.

"Back in the 1850s," she said, "when a man named Brace,

Charles Loring Brace, came to New York, he was appalled by the numbers—and they were in the thousands—of homeless children roaming the streets of the city. He saw them dressed in rags, sleeping huddled in doorways, rummaging through garbage for food, poor, starving, miserable little creatures. He decided to do something about the situation, and in time he founded the Children's Aid Society.

"He set up a plan to send those children who were not diseased out of the city to rural areas, where they would be given homes either by couples with no children of their own, or by families who were anxious to take in young boys and girls to help with the work on the farms. Agents are sent out periodically to check on the children, to see that they attend school, and that they are not abused or taken advantage of in any way."

"But suppose the farmers don't want any strange children, what then?" I asked.

"Not all of them do, of course," she replied, "but the plan has worked surprisingly well. If all of the children in a group are not placed in a town, they are taken on to the next one. I know about this, because we at the Foundling have sent some of our older children, ones who have no chance of being adopted here, and of course we've had reports on them. We have to move some of them out, Maida, otherwise we'd be woefully overcrowded, like so many of the city orphanages."

"You wouldn't send Christina, would you?" I asked.

"No, indeed. Your brother and his wife will adopt her formally as soon as they return from Europe. Don't worry, Christina is safe. She's one of the fortunate ones."

"I wish I could live with Jerome and Maria," I said, "but that—"

"No, even if they were here, that would be too close to what you ran away from, Maida," she said quickly, "at least for the present. Perhaps later on."

We were quiet for a few moments, and then she looked at me and spoke seriously.

"If you accept this position, Maida, I know you will do it well. You are so good with children! It won't be a lifetime job, you know, but it will get you out of the city when that is of paramount importance. I understand there is a train leaving for Michigan tomorrow with a group. The Society has agreed to put you up for tonight—I am afraid to keep you at the Foundling any longer—and you will be given tickets, instructions, everything you need before you leave tomorrow."

"But, Sister, I don't know anything about—"

"You mustn't worry, my dear. There will be another agent traveling with you, an experienced gentleman."

The cab drew up just then in front of 24 St. Mark's Place, and she leaned forward to kiss me on the forehead.

"Remember that you are Mary Wicklow now, not Maida Jardine," she said with a smile. "I'll say good-bye to you here, my dear. Take this satchel; I've packed some extra clothing for you. Ask for Mrs. Carstairs when you go in. She is expecting you."

"Sister, how can I thank you?" I felt tears pricking my eyes as I spoke.

"Write to me when you have a chance," she answered, "and telephone when you return from this trip. Good-bye, my dear, and God bless you."

It was many months before I wrote to her, long after our ten charges had been placed in homes in or around the small town of Redfield, Michigan. For children who had been rescued from the city streets, they were remarkably well-behaved, and once their rags had been exchanged for the warm winter clothing provided by the Children's Aid Society, they could have passed for the progeny of any middle-class family.

I still have a picture of the group, taken just before we

boarded the train on the morning of the seventeenth. In the front row the four-year-old twins, Nellie and Louann, are smiling shyly, while alongside them the four youngest boys, Joseph, Billy, Mike, and Tommy, stand almost at attention, looking apprehensive, but trying to smile. In the row behind them the four older children, ranging in age from eight to ten, stare seriously at the camera. No smiles there, and young Roger, at the extreme right, is obviously struggling to hold back his tears.

Mr. Brookfield, the other agent, and I stand behind the children. He is a tall, gray-haired man, and his face is open and kindly-looking. Mine is barely visible; at the last minute I had pulled down the veil on my hat as far as it would go, in case the picture should appear in a newspaper.

Thank goodness Mr. B., as the children called him (I became known only as Miss Mary), knew exactly what had to be done and when to do it. On that long, tiring train trip he took complete charge of the six boys, while I looked after the four girls. The two older ones, Peggy and Sal, were no trouble at all, but the twins demanded attention, and needed constant reassurance that nothing bad was going to happen to them. According to Mrs. Carstairs, the poor little things had been found cowering in the corner of a filthy room next to the corpse of their mother. They mentioned a man named Paulie, but did not know whether he was their father or not, and the Society had been unable to trace him.

"They are not to be separated," Mrs. Carstairs had warned us before we left. "They need each other, and there's something so endearing about them that I am sure some childless couple will snap them up. Just keep them happy on the trip."

It wasn't difficult to amuse them during the day, but I found it anything but comfortable at night to try to sleep while sitting up in the coach with one twin on my lap and the other snuggled up against me. (What a far cry from Mr. Bradley's private railroad car!) It was a relief when the train pulled into the station at Redfield, Michigan, two and a half days later.

"The villagers will put us up for the first night, Miss Mary," Mr. B. explained, "probably on cots set up in the depot, and the next day we will all go to the church. After the service I will explain the rules and regulations to the congregation—how the children are to be cared for, their education seen to, and so on. After that the people will make their choices."

"And if some children are not chosen, then we go on to the next town?" I asked.

"Yes," he answered, "probably Appleton in this case. But I don't think that will be necessary; we have a particularly nice-looking group with us on this trip."

They did look nice when we got off the train, with their winter coats buttoned up to their necks, their caps and bonnets straight, and any grubby fingers hidden in woolen mittens. As I stood on the gravel in front of the station, holding a twin by each hand and keeping Peggy and Sal close to me, I saw eager smiles on the faces of several women who were approaching us from the row of farm wagons lined up near the tracks. They were so bundled up against the cold that it was impossible to tell what manner of clothing they wore under the heavy shawls and cloaks, but they looked neatly groomed and kindly enough, I thought, if somewhat colorless, blending into the dull grays and browns of the town itself.

From where I stood I could see six or seven weather-beaten wooden buildings behind a row of tall trees, leafless now under the gray winter sky. A large general store stood between a bank and a barroom, but I turned away without trying to identify the other buildings, feeling somewhat oppressed by the dreary face Redfield presented.

Mr. B. was making a short speech about the meeting to be held in the church the next day, and when he finished we were all herded into the station, where four or five women wearing denim aprons stood behind a long table, ready to ladle out soup and serve corn fritters. I don't know when I relished a meal so much; on the train we'd had only sandwiches, apples, and cold water to sustain us.

Since there were only eleven cots lined up against the walls of the the station, poor Mr. B. had to sleep on one of the benches, but when he rose in the morning he was as cheerful as if he'd slept on the finest of mattresses. I straightened as many of the rumpled clothes as I could (we hadn't been able to undress since leaving New York), brushed heads of hair, and washed the hands and faces of the girls while Mr. B. supervised the grooming of the boys.

At nine o'clock the same women who had provided our meal the night before arrived with baskets of homemade bread, jars of jam, a pail of milk for the children, and a pot of coffee for Mr. B. and me. The last woman to come in carried a laundry basket filled with cups, most of them tin and a few of thick white china, as well as an assortment of plates and spoons, which she quickly set out on the table we had used the previous evening. The bread was still warm, and when I commented on how good it tasted with the jam on it, I was told that that was just Maisie's wildberry preserves, nothing special.

Maisie was the only name I learned, and I never did find out which one she was. Apparently introductions were unimportant to these women, or else they were shy. I made a mental note to ask Mr. B. about that later. I had no time to talk to him then; as soon as we'd eaten I was scrubbing faces again, buttoning up coats, and locating mittens and hats in preparation for our appearance in public.

The small white church on one side of the village green—really just an open field—was crowded, and the children, jammed against each other in the rear pews, were understandably restless during the service. But when the final hymn had been sung and the pastor announced that Mr. B. would speak to the congregation, they became nervously attentive. The excitement of the trip was over and they were to be separated, their futures placed in the hands of strangers in a part of the country far away from anything they had ever known.

Little Nellie crawled up onto my lap, while her twin clung to my arm, and when Louann asked in a whisper if I couldn't keep them, I almost cried. I couldn't tell her that my own future was even more uncertain than hers; all I could do was to give her a hug and kiss her eager little face.

"And now," Mr. B. was saying, "if you will give us a few minutes, we will line the children up outside, where you will be able to look them over and make your choices."

As if they were cattle for sale, I thought, ushering my charges out into the cold, gray day. And indeed the speculative looks in the eyes of some of the Redfield residents seemed to indicate that the children were being judged on the basis of their future usefulness about the farms, rather than on their need of a home.

The selection process did not take long; the older boys were quickly chosen by farmers who promised to feed, clothe, and educate them in exchange for simple chores. Papers were signed, and the boys were driven off in wagons, sometimes without any farewells. To my surprise Peggy and Sal were placed almost immediately in adjacent farms. "That way they'll be able to visit each other, miss," a sturdy-looking housewife said to me, "and it won't be so lonesome for them." A considerate woman, she.

When I looked around, Mr. B. was arranging for the last of the younger boys to be taken by an elderly couple who wanted a companion for their grandson. I had been more concerned about young Roger than about the others; he was a quiet child, pale and small for his age, always on the edge, as it were, watching the other boys instead of joining in any of the little games they played on the train. Several times he left them to sit on the floor in front of me and listen to the story I was telling the twins, never taking his eyes from my face.

"Willie is just your age, son," I heard the grandfather say. "The two of you will go to school together, play in the barn, feed the chickens. You'll get along fine." I could only hope they would.

A light snow had begun to fall, and I felt inexpressibly lonely standing on the cold ground, with the twins clinging disconsolately to my skirts, the only children left.

"Over here, Miss Mary," Mr. B. called, as young Roger went off with the elderly couple. "I want you to meet Mr. and Mrs. Miller, who are interested in giving the twins a home, and adopting them eventually if things work out."

I liked the looks of the Millers at once. She was a pretty, slender young woman who radiated warmth as she bent down to talk to the little girls, while he, a giant of a fellow, stood watching her, smiling and nodding his head. There was a sweetness about her, and a solid strength about him, which the twins must have sensed intuitively, because a short time later he had one on each arm and they were waving good-bye to me, all tears forgotten.

"They'll be fine, Miss Mary," Mr. B. said as we watched the last wagon disappear. "The Millers are a childless couple, and they need Nellie and Louann as much as the little ones need a home.

"It all went very well, I think; no one left over this time. These are good people here in Redfield. I'm not worried about any one of the children, but of course we'll send someone to check up on them in a couple of months."

The snow, which up until then had been no more than light flurries, now began to come down steadily.

"Well, we can't just stand here," I said somewhat impatiently. "Shouldn't we go to the station and wait for the train back to New York?"

"There's no train until tomorrow morning," he replied, taking my arm. "But come, we'll take cover in the station anyway. I believe lodging for the night has been arranged for us, but just where—oh, this must be our host now."

A wagon driven by a man so wrapped up against the weather that little more than his eyes were visible came into view and clattered to a halt beside us.

"Sorry to be late," shouted the driver. "Trouble with an axle. Hop in, hop in. Good food and a warm fire waitin' for you at home. Hold on, miss. All ready, sir? Settin' in for a big snow, looks like."

I cannot say it was a comfortable ride, but fortunately it was a short one, and inside of fifteen minutes we were in the yard of a prosperous-looking farm.

"In you go, miss—here, take my arm. Momma and Poppa are waitin' for you. Name's Iverson, by the way. Vern Iverson. Here they are, Momma!"

"Lower your voice, Vern!" admonished the plump, rosy-cheeked woman who came to the door. "You'd wear the ears off a brass monkey. He can't seem to talk soft, miss; Doc Hansen says it's because his hearin' ain't so good. Here, come over to the stove and warm yourself. Take off those wet coats. Vern, bring in some more wood. Poppa, where'd you get to? Come here and—oh, there you are."

A tall man with a lean brown face came in from some other part of the house, nodded to us, and sat down at the end of the large wooden table in the center of the kitchen. Apparently the Iversons had no more use for formal introductions than the women who had fed us at the station. Mrs. Iverson chattered on, seldom waiting for an answer, all the while bustling around the kitchen, moving from stove to cupboard to table with an ease and efficiency that came from long practice.

"Sakes alive," she exclaimed suddenly, "what have I been thinkin' of? You'll be wantin' to wash up, miss, and you, mister. Vern, watch that nothin' burns while I show them their rooms."

With that she ushered us out of the warm kitchen into a drafty hall and up a steep flight of stairs.

"Nothin' fancy here, miss," she said apologetically, opening the door to a small, cold bedroom, "but it's all clean, and plenty of bedclothes. I told the pastor so when he asked us to take you in, when he said we should do our share, seein' as we weren't takin' no orphans."

"We're most grateful," I began.

"Not that I wouldn't have liked to take a little one. Gets lonesome here at times, but Arnold, he was dead set against it. Said if he couldn't have more of his own childer he wouldn't have someone else's. There, miss: water's in the pitcher, so's you can wash your hands and face. Chamber pot's in the closet, case you need it in the night. Privy's out back. Thank the Lord, Arnold built a covered way out to it; in this weather it'd be no fun gettin' to it through the snow. Mister, you're just down the hall; yes, that's your door. Now I'll leave you to clean up. But don't take long, dinner's almost ready to put on the table."

Thank heavens this is only for one night, I thought, looking around the sparsely furnished, unheated bedroom, which had a stale smell about it, as if it had been closed off for some time. Besides the bed it boasted a single straight-backed chair, an old-fashioned washstand, over which a cracked mirror hung crookedly, and a small braided rug.

The "closet" mentioned by Mrs. Iverson consisted of a series of hooks lined up on one wall, only partially hidden by a faded gingham curtain. I shivered as I washed my hands and face in water that wasn't even tepid, and for the first time since leaving the Fifth Avenue house I thought longingly of the comforts I had taken for granted all my life: the hot, scented baths, the soft, monogrammed towels, the comfortable warmth of my own bedroom.

Now that the terror of my last night in my parents' house had receded somewhat, I began to question the wisdom of my flight from Fifth Avenue, and to wonder if, one way or another, a reconcilation with my mother might be brought about. When she learned how Viscount Ormley had threatened to violate me, would she not see him for what he was? Would she not be frantic with worry about my safety, and welcome me back with open arms? Somewhere I had read about the overpowering strength of the maternal instinct . . .

The loud ringing of a bell—a cowbell, I learned later—startled me, and after a glance in the cracked mirror I hurried down to the warmth of the kitchen. Platters of meat, potatoes, and turnips were set out in front of Mr. Iverson, whose clothing, I noticed as I took my place, smelled strongly of something unfamiliar to me. A barn smell, I decided.

A bowl of gravy, a plate of thick-sliced bread, and a dish of butter occupied the center of the table. After saying a lengthy grace, Mr. Iverson served everyone exactly the same portions: two slices of meat, and two spoonfuls each of the vegetables. Then the gravy, bread, and butter were passed around the table in rapid succession. The meat, pork with a pungent sweet-sour taste, was deliciously tender, but the potatoes were lumpy, and I had to cover the turnips with gravy in order to make them palatable. Except for an occasional request for more bread or butter, no one spoke until Mrs. Iverson rose to clear the plates and take an enormous deep-dish pie from the oven.

"Dried apple pie's all we got now," she said, cutting a large wedge and passing it to her husband. "Nothin' like a fresh green apple pie, but—"

"Better'n rice puddin', anyway," boomed Vern, handing a plate to Mr. B. and smiling across the table at me.

Far better than rice pudding, I thought, savoring the spicy flavor of the apples and the flaky crust, but suddenly I was not only satiated but also unutterably tired. A wave of exhaustion enveloped me, and only with a great effort did I manage to sit through the final grace.

"Miss Mary, are you not well?" Mr. B. asked anxiously. "You look—"

"The poor girl's wore out," Mrs. Iverson interrupted, "and no wonder, with all them childer to care for and travelin' so far. Go along up to your bed, miss, and have a nice rest. There's a patchwork quilt on the shelf of your closet. Put that over you."

As I stood up to leave the table, I noticed the master of the house was staring at me intently, and wondered whether he disapproved of someone's lying down in the middle of the afternoon. It wasn't exactly a friendly look I saw in his eyes, but more like one of appraisal, as if he were inspecting me. I shivered slightly and headed for the stairs.

I couldn't wait to get out of the clothes I had worn steadily for the past few days, and even though I knew I'd have to put most of them on again for supper, I undressed completely and pulled on the flannel nightgown Sister Mary Vee had packed. When I slipped in between the icy sheets my feet felt so cold that a few minutes later I jumped up again and put on a pair of thick black woolen stockings, the kind I had seen the nuns wear at the Foundling. I must look a picture, I thought, but I'm too tired to care.

"Seemed a pity to wake you for supper," Mrs. Iverson said the next morning when I appeared in the kitchen. "Mr. B. said, too, to let you sleep, seein' as you'd not had a good night's rest since leavin' the East. Sit right down, miss. Here's porridge, and I'll have your eggs ready when you've put that away. That's one thing we have plenty of, fresh eggs."

The good woman busied herself at the great black stove, keeping up a steady stream of talk about the cold, the snow, and the "useless" black-and-white cat named Olaf that did nothing but sleep and eat all day, while I concentrated on a rather glutinous bowl of cereal. Brown sugar helped, but not much. After she had set a plate of crispy bacon and two perfectly fried eggs in front of me, she poured coffee from the large enamel pot on the back of the stove and sat down at the table to talk.

"My, it does me good to have comp'ny!" She sighed happily. "Days can be long here, 'specially in winter. Looks like you'll be here for a spell, too. Arnold says the snow's four, five feet deep, not countin' the drifts."

"Where is he?" I asked, "and where is Mr. B.?"

"Out to the barn," she replied. "Good thing Vern got the ropes up last night—"

"Ropes? What—"

"To hold on to, miss. In storms like this you could lose your way just steppin' outside. The ropes go from the house door to the barn, an' the men just hang on to them."

I gathered that Vern and Mr. Iverson had to tend to the livestock, and that Mr. B. went along to see if he could be of help. He didn't strike me as the kind of man who would know much about cows and pigs and chickens and whatever other animals the Iversons raised, but perhaps he'd been brought up on a farm.

"They'll be in for a warm-up, wantin' coffee and cake," she said, wincing as she rose from the table. "Ach, my leg is bad today. Seems the cold weather brings on the rheumatics."

I helped her set out plates, cups, and two platters of some kind of Swedish cakes that looked a little like crullers, and then wandered over to the two rocking chairs that had been placed at either end of a braided rug in front of a window. The snow was still coming down steadily, and when I realized that I could see only a few feet into the distance, I was afraid it might be days, even weeks, before I'd be on a train back to a world I knew, a world I now missed desperately.

"Take them boots off right there!" I heard Mrs. Iverson command as the door burst open and three snow-covered figures stamped into the kitchen, "and hang up yer coats next to the stove. Coffee's hot. Sit down, sit down."

"Brought in some eggs, Momma," Vern shouted, putting a covered basket down on the table. "I could eat half a dozen right now if you'll fix 'em."

"How can I fix eggs for you when I'm startin' dinner?" she retorted. "Eat the cakes and quiet down."

Does she ever stop cooking? I wondered silently, feeling as useless as Olaf. I was glad when Mr. B. sat down in the other rocker and asked me if I'd had a good sleep. I nodded, and then told him I'd been wondering how the orphans were adjusting to their new homes.

"Probably the older boys have been given chores to keep them busy," he said, crossing his legs and rocking gently, "and even the younger ones will be assigned little jobs. In any case, they'll be warm and dry, and far better off than they were on the streets of New York."

"The twins have each other," I said, "and the Millers looked like the kind of people who would keep them happy, but, Mr. B., I worry about Peggy and Sal. It could be a lonesome time for them."

"No, you mustn't worry, Miss Mary. There's always work to be done in a farmhouse. Look how Mrs. Iverson is kept busy cooking. Probably Peggy and Sal are learning how to bake bread or peel potatoes."

"I wish I could do something like that," I said. "I feel as if I'm in the way here, and the time passes so slowly."

"You've done your job, Miss Mary. Just rest up," he said soothingly. "We'll be out of here before you know it."

The day dragged on and on and on, with the men making trips to the barn, Mrs. Iverson cooking and drinking coffee (how did she stand it?) and chattering away about churning butter, salting meat, making sauerkraut, and so on.

"Oh, don't think I'm complainin', miss," she said, glancing up from the dough she was kneading. "Winter cookin' is nothin' to what I have to do the rest of the year. Spring, summer, and fall, that's when it's hard; that's when the hired men are back for the plantin' and the hayin' and the harvestin' and what have you. Have to work hard in this country; foreclosures all over the place. An' then there's the crew that works in the orchards, apple trees needin' prunin' and all that. You want a good crop, it takes work, the pickin' an' packin' and haulin' to the depot to be shipped off to Detroit. Our apples is prizes, that they are, but oh! cookin' for all them men is no easy thing—and can they eat!"

She paused for breath, and looked thoughtful for a moment.

"Arnold says he'll get me a girl to help, but I don't know that they're much good. Might not be such a good idea anyway; some of them girls is a big temptation to have around."

A temptation for Vern, I supposed she meant as I watched her put the bread in the oven and close the door.

"There," she said with a sigh of relief. "Now I can set for a while, rest these old legs."

She sat down in the rocker, and I waited for her to go on talking, but after pulling a shawl around her shoulders she dozed off, and except for the gentle hiss of a pot on the stove and the ticking of an old banjo clock on the wall, the kitchen was blessedly quiet.

Later, much later, when the final meal of the day was over—a supper of potato salad, cold ham, corn bread, cheese, and custard pudding—and the kitchen cleaned up, I excused myself, and taking a candle from the row on the dresser, went up to my cold bedroom and even colder sheets. I lay awake for a while, listening to the sounds of the boards settling. Vern had told me that they contract in extremely cold weather, and said I mustn't be frightened if I sometimes heard a loud snap, like a branch breaking.

My mind drifted back to my old life, and I wondered what I would do if I ever did get back to New York again. Where would I go? Would I dare approach Mother? Perhaps, I thought, I ought to see Sister Mary Vee first, and find out if she had seen my parents. I really didn't want to be sent on another orphan train—oh, if only Jerome were home! Then I could live with him, and work at the Foundling . . .

I had just settled down to sleep after deciding that the first thing for me to do would be to get in touch with Father at his bank, when I heard a noise unlike any contraction of boards and realized that my bedroom door was being slowly and carefully opened.

I had read somewhere that fright sometimes paralyzes the vocal chords, a statement I believe to be true, for I could no more have screamed or called out at that moment than I could have flown out the window.

I fumbled for the matches I had left on the washstand, and by the time I got the candle lighted, the door was closed again. The noise I made groping for the matches had probably alerted whoever was out there that I was awake. Or could a draft have caused the door to open and then close again? Then I detected a faint odor, faint but distinguishable as the odor Arnold Iverson carried around with him.

There was no key for that bedroom door, and when I looked around for something to put against it, my glance fell on the straight-backed chair. In no time at all I was wedging its top rung under the doorknob, the way Jerome used to do when the key to his room was lost. I climbed back into bed and blew out the candle, but it was a long time before I fell asleep.

I said nothing about the night's incident the next morning at breakfast, thinking that poor Mrs. Iverson had enough to contend with. Vern was his usual loud self, and Mr. B., cheered by the news that the snow was tapering off, was unusually talkative. Only Mr. Iverson looked annoyed. He ate little, and left the table as the rest of us were starting on our ham and eggs. His wife shook her head in exasperation and put his plate on the back of the stove. Then she launched into stories of past storms, all of which were far worse than what we had seen in the past two days. It all seemed so comfortable and cozy, so perfectly ordinary, that I was almost able to convince myself that I had imagined the smell, that the door had swung open of its own accord, or that I hadn't closed it properly to begin with.

Later in the morning, however, I changed my mind. When I was returning from the outdoor toilet I heard voices raised in the kitchen, and paused behind the door that led out to the covered way.

"It's as plain as the nose on your face what you were up to, Arnold Iverson," the farmer's wife said angrily. "I heard you git up in the night, and it wasn't to go down to the privy that you went. I'd've heard you on the stairs as you went down. Can't leave a young girl alone, can you? Well—"

"Mind your mouth, woman—"

"And don't pretend you don't know why I let that hired girl go last summer—"

The sound of a blow being struck and her cry of pain, followed by a muttered oath, caused me to retreat to the privy, where I stood shivering until I heard the outer door slam. The kitchen, which had seemed like such a safe haven a few hours before, had turned into a battlefield, and except for Olaf, an empty one when I returned to it. The large cat followed me over to the window and jumped up on my lap when I sank into one of the rocking chairs. Olaf purred contentedly while I tried to think of the best way to protect myself during the coming night. Would the chair hold? It was not a particularly sturdy piece of furniture, and strong pressure, such as Mr. Iverson was capable of exerting, could easily shatter the top rung. If that happened, I thought, I would simply scream my head off until . . .

At that point Mr. B. came back from the barn with the news that Vern was working on the sleigh, and would have it ready to take us to the station in time for the train the next morning. Good news indeed, but there was still a night to get through.

"Better pack up tonight, Miss Mary, and be ready to leave

at daybreak." Vern's voice boomed across the kitchen. "Train comes at seven or thereabouts. Where's Momma gone? I need to eat."

He went over to the stove and was lifting up pot covers when his mother came in from the hallway, looking perfectly normal. Her husband must have hit her someplace where it didn't show.

It didn't take me long to pack the clothes Sister Mary Vee had put in the satchel and the few things I had packed in Aunt Eulalia's handbag, including the envelope of money Father had given me. That had been left untouched. Somewhere along the line I had counted the bills, and was surprised that they amounted to one hundred and fifty-five dollars, a large sum for anyone to carry around. I counted it once more, then returned it to the handbag, which I placed next to me on the bed in case I needed to swing it as I had done once before.

Nothing did happen to disturb me that night, though, and in the morning I wondered if Mrs. Iverson had lain awake all through the dark hours keeping an eye on her husband. Perhaps she had—or maybe she had tied him to the bedpost.

Over Mr. B.'s protests I engaged a bedroom on the train for the trip back to the city. After the stress of the past two nights I had no desire to spend two more sitting up. He insisted on traveling coach himself, but he did come in to sit with me from time to time during the day. He was either without curiosity or else extremely reserved, for he never asked me how I could afford such a luxury, or anything about my private life. Nor did I feel it necessary to volunteer any information concerning my appointment as an agent. I did, however, tell him what Mr. Iverson had done.

"Although the possibility of a young girl's being placed there seems remote, shouldn't the Children's Aid Society be made aware of the situation?" I asked, glancing at his shocked expression.

"Good Lord, yes!" he exclaimed. "Do you mean to say he—I had no idea—were you terribly frightened? Oh, dear me, yes indeed, the Society shall hear of this."

He sat quietly for a moment or two, and then continued.

"One good thing, though, is that Redfield will not be on the list for some time to come. If I recall correctly, the next group is to go to Kansas, and the one after that to Iowa. But nevertheless, what you have told me shall go on record."

Shortly after that conversation he left me, and I did not see him again until the trip was nearly over.

"Here's a New York paper for you, Miss Mary," he said cheerfully. "A boy came through with them at the last station. Thought you might like to see it. We'll be there in a little over an hour. I imagine you're getting anxious to see your family and friends, eh?"

I smiled and nodded, thinking that in my case the word "anxious" did not mean what he thought it did. After he left I sat back and glanced at the headlines. I saw nothing of particular interest to me at first, but when I turned to the second page, the words leaped out at me.

VISCOUNT HOVERS BETWEEN LIFE AND DEATH

ATTACKER STILL AT LARGE

If he dies I'll be responsible, I thought. I knew I had left him lying on the kitchen floor the night I ran away, left him bleeding, and if he should die, it would be my fault. Only when I read the rest of the newspaper article did I calm down a bit. Apparently the authorities were blaming the attack on the viscount on an intruder:

Since the service door of the Jardine mansion was found to be partially open, it is thought to be the means through which the assailant gained entry. No valuables are missing, and it is assumed that after attacking the viscount, the intruder was frightened off when he heard footsteps on the back stairs. Mr. Jardine, upon hearing noises in the kitchen, descended the stairs and found the viscount lying on the floor. Viscount Ormley, the only son of the Earl of Delcannon, had been on an extended visit to New York. The earl has offered a substantial reward for information leading to the capture of the culprit. "No punishment is too severe," the earl said, "for one dastardly enough to inflict such a brutal wound on my son, and should he die, I will see his murderer hanged."

The viscount is still unable to speak. He was said to be engaged to be married to Miss Maida Jardine, who is wanted for questioning.

At the mention of my name my heart began to thump wildly. I could still see the blood flowing from the blow I had dealt him with my handbag. Perhaps he has lost so much blood that he will die, I thought, and if I say nothing at all about having seen Ormley on my way out, no one will ever know that I did it. But could I keep what happened in the kitchen that night to myself for the rest of my life? If the supposed intruder was never found and punished, I wouldn't have anything to worry about, would I?

Oh, what's the use? I thought. Would anyone ever believe me?

I put the newspaper aside after returning it to its original folds, and tried to decide where to go first. Certainly not to the Children's Aid Society, since they might have my real name on record. And not to the Foundling Hospital; I couldn't involve

Sister Mary Vee any further in my affairs when there was a possibility of my being a crime suspect. Nor could I face any member of my family—they'd probably disown me. Maybe Father wouldn't . . .

I would have to hide. I would have to find a place to live and some means of support, since Father's money wouldn't last forever. I remembered that he said to write to him at the bank if I needed funds, and that was comforting, but at the time the necessity of remaining out of sight seemed all-important.

When the train pulled into Pennsylvania Station I said a hurried farewell to Mr. B., pretending I was eager to see my family, and slipped away into the crowd before he could say anything about reporting to 24 St. Mark's Place. He smiled and waved cheerfully, as if we were destined to meet again soon, and we went our separate ways.

Part Two

chapter nine

Three days later I was sitting on the bed in the two-dollars-a-week room I had rented in a house on Bleecker Street, counting what remained of my money and trying to stop crying. The landlady, a Mrs. Erdmann, had said the room was a bargain at that price, but I didn't think much of it. It wasn't even as large as the bedroom at the Iversons's farm, and not nearly as clean. It did have a real closet, and there was a bathroom (of sorts) down the hall. The only word I could think of that suited it, though, was dismal, which was exactly how I felt.

My head ached, my feet were sore from the miles of pavement and cobblestones I had covered in a fruitless search for employment, and my funds were diminishing. Also, although my picture had not appeared in any of the newspapers I bought each morning, I lived in fear of being recognized. Interest in the viscount seemed to be fading; only once did I come across a short paragraph saying he was in critical condition and still unable to describe his assailant.

Miserable though I was, I could not bring myself to appeal for help to anyone connected with my former life. I was too afraid of being arrested for murder, or attempted murder. Even though the police thought a burglar had injured the viscount, would they not reason thus, I asked myself:

1. Maida Jardine was being forced into a marriage against her will.

2. On the night of February 14, the viscount called on the Jardines to make a formal proposal.

3. The next night the viscount was found almost dead of a head wound in the Jardine kitchen.

4. Maida Jardine disappeared that same night and is wanted for questioning.

But would they necessarily know all that? What would Mother and Father have told them about me? There was so much I didn't know.

Father would help me, he had said he would, and Jerome surely would; he must be coming back from Europe soon, I thought. How can I involve them, though? How can I ask them to cover up what I have done? I have committed a crime, and will have to live with that knowledge, so it's better that I stay out of their lives. Maybe I should have stayed in Michigan and married Vern, I thought ruefully. I wiped my eyes, and had just lighted the single gas jet the room afforded when someone knocked on my door.

"Hope I'm not disturbing you—I saw you come in a little while ago—could you fasten this darn hook for me? Oh, you've been crying! What's the trouble?" asked the pretty, somewhat breathless young woman who stood in the doorway. Without waiting for an answer she came further into the room and looked at me closely.

"Oh, my," she said, "you're far too pretty to be cryin'.

Now look, my pa always said food helps make you feel better. Fasten me up, and come out and have a meal and tell me about it."

"Who are you?" I asked hesitantly. "Do you live here?"

"Right across the hall, dearie. Name's Rose, Rose Reiner. Two r's. I was never a hand at all three of them. I think it was 'rithmetic that did me in. Come, put on your hat and coat while I get mine. What's your name?"

"Mary Wick—" I stopped abruptly, thinking I'd better not use the name by which the Children's Aid Society knew me.

"Mary Wick," she said with a laugh. "That's an easy one to remember. Ready? Let's go."

Over a meal in a cheap but clean little eating place on Mercer Street she told me she'd come to New York from a small town upstate to better herself.

"Nothin' ever happens in Broadville—really shoulda been called Narrowville—nothin'. You have to wait for someone to die before you can get a halfway decent job, and the only men there aren't worth thinkin' about, just farmers always cryin' poor. Chances are better here. What about you? Where're you from?"

I quickly made up a story about having been brought up by my grandmother out in eastern Long Island, both my parents having died when I was a baby.

"And now she's gone, too," I went on, surprised at my own glibness. "Poor old soul, she was sick for so long that the medicines and the doctor bills ate up all her savings. And then they foreclosed on the mortgage . . ." I pretended to wipe away a tear.

"So you were left alone, Mary? Have you found work yet?" Rose asked.

"No, and I've looked all over. No one wants me. One lady almost hired me as a parlormaid, but when she heard I'd had no experience she changed her mind."

"Oh, you wouldn't want to be a maid!" Rose exclaimed. "That's a terrible life. I tried it once; lasted a week." She paused for a moment and looked at me thoughtfully.

"Maybe," she said slowly, "maybe I could get you in at Triangle."

"What's Triangle?"

"It's a shirtwaist company, where all them Gibson girl shirtwaists are made. It's in the Ashe Building, over on Greene Street, near Washington Square. Hundreds of girls work there, and someone's always leaving. Let me see—yeah, whyn't you come in with me in the morning, and I'll interduce you to Dinah Lipschitz. She's in charge of our shop, hands out all the work and that—"

"But, Rose, I haven't any idea how to make a shirtwaist."

Rose laughed. "Neither had I," she said. "Still don't. All you have to do is sew the same seam over and over again. Any idiot could do it, and believe me, there are plenty of idiots there. Give it a try, Mary. You don't have to stay if something better turns up."

The next morning at eight o'clock I stood with Rose in front of a long table on the tenth floor of the Ashe Building, where a harried-looking woman was counting piles of what looked like parts of blouses.

"Rose Reiner, you're a godsend!" she exclaimed after my friend had told her I was looking for work. "How did you know that Celia Weintraub left without warning yesterday at closing time? So we're short—what's your name again? Mary Wick? Take her along, Rose, and show her Celia's machine— yes, yes! I'm coming! Hold your horses!"

"Does this mean I'm hired?" I asked Rose as I followed her down a narrow hall.

"Yes, silly," she answered, smiling. "And you'll be only two machines away from me, in case you need help."

I needed plenty of help that first day, but Rose was patient, and the girl on my right, Josephine Nicolini, a tall girl with soft brown eyes, evidently thought I needed encouragement. She'd look up from her own work from time to time to smile and nod at me.

"You did real good for your first day," she said when the bell rang at four forty-five. "Only five sleeves in the trash bin. My first day I ruined ten of them. You must have used a machine before."

"Yes, but not like this one. My grandmother was a seamstress, and she showed me," I lied, thinking of the doll clothes old Miss Crippleby had helped me make.

When we reached the exit on Greene Street I was surprised to see that a man stood under the time clock examining each girl's pocketbook or handbag as she left. I thought he looked puzzled at the size of Aunt Eulalia's gift, but he said nothing. Later on I bought a cheap purse to carry, and left the ugly thing on the shelf of my closet. I should have thrown it out.

"What on earth do they think we'd steal?" I asked Rose as we made our way out to the street. She hushed me quickly, and didn't reply until we were away from the crowd coming out of the building.

"Some people'll steal anything, dearie. Maybe Mama needs a new needle for her machine, or a bobbin, or a spool of thread, something like that. Too difficult to hide any material in a purse, and no chance of taking any money. They never leave that around. I hope you didn't leave any in your room, did you?"

"Yes, but I sewed it into the waistband of my other skirt."

"Oh my God! I hope it's still there. Old Erdmann is a snoop, and of course she has keys to all the rooms."

The money hadn't been touched, but our landlady may have looked for it. At least I thought I noticed a slight odor of patchouli perfume in the room, which certainly did not come from any of my few possessions.

The next day I wore my "other" skirt to work.

*   *   *

Although I was grateful to be gainfully employed (but since the pay was only eight dollars a week, "gainfully" is hardly the right word to use here), I cannot say I ever enjoyed a single day I spent in the Triangle establishment. The work was monotonous, exacting, and tiring, the noise of the machines deafening, and the air dusty and stale. I kept telling myself that no one would ever look for me on the tenth floor of the Ashe Building, and that I'd better stay, at least until the end of the week, or maybe until the end of the month, before looking for a better position in more congenial surroundings. By the time the month of March ended, however, I was in no condition to work anyplace.

Rose probably would have been hurt had she had any inkling of my plans to leave, but she never knew about them. During the short time I'd been at Triangle we'd become good, but not intimate, friends, and I missed her when she was suddenly called upon to return home to help care for her parents, both of whom had become ill.

"I don't know when I'll ever get a chance to come back," she moaned the night before she left. "I don't want to go, but you know how it is. You didn't leave your grandmother when she got sick—and they wouldn't send for me if they had anyone else to turn to. Write to me, Mary. Just send the letters to Rose Reiner, Broadville, New York. I'll miss you."

I was surprised at how much I missed her, the meals we had shared, the walks to and from work, the evenings we had spent together, washing our hair, mending our clothes, never anything exciting, just companionable. After her departure my evenings seemed long and empty. I tried to fill them in by taking little walks around the neighborhood after a solitary meal before going up to my room. I bought a newspaper regularly, and scanned it for any information about the Ormley case, but I came across no further references to it. He couldn't have died, then, I thought; I hope he's gone back to England. On the society page of the *Tribune,* however, I read that Mr. and Mrs. Julian Jardine had left New York for an extended visit to Palm Beach, where they proposed to build a house on the waterfront. I wondered how Father was . . .

The motherly Josephine must have sensed that I was lonely, because on a Friday, I remember it was St. Patrick's Day, she invited me to her home for dinner.

"Of course we're not Irish, Mary," she said. "Not with a name like Nicolini. But my mama is a great one for celebrating a saint's day, any saint, doesn't matter which one. She'll cook up enough food for the whole parade, most likely."

"Don't be surprised at the size of my family," Josephine warned me as we set out after work. "There's Mama and Papa—he's a bookkeeper—and Tony, the oldest, then me, then Camilla, and Anna, and after them Luigi—such a tease—then Pauli, and Silvio, the baby. He's just two."

"Seven children! What a nice family!" I exclaimed, and stopped myself just in time from saying that there'd been six in my own family. "And you all live at home?"

"Where else?" she laughed. "But Tony's talking about joining the Navy, and maybe in another year Roberto and I will have saved up enough to marry on."

"Josephine, how exciting! I didn't know you were engaged."

"Well, I have no ring. He wants to buy me one, but I tell him it's better to save the money for a wedding ring. And we'll be needin' other things. You'll like him, Mary; he's comin' over after dinner. His mama wants him home for meals most days."

It was a cold, windy walk from the Triangle building down to Mulberry Street, but no welcome could have been warmer than the one that greeted us on our arrival at the small house in Little Italy.

"Ah, Josie, you've brought her, your beautiful friend!" Mrs. Nicolini was a short, cheerful woman with bright black eyes and a welcoming smile. "No, no, Silvio! Don't put your sticky hands on the lady's skirt! Come in, come in! Tony, take her coat! Come, warm yourself."

When I think back now on that happy, noisy evening, with the baby wanting to sit on my lap and the other children clustering around me, I remember the wonderful spicy aroma that drifted out from the kitchen, and that I felt as if I had stumbled into a warm, comfortable haven, far away from the workaday world.

"What have you done to Luigi, Mary?" Camilla asked with a chuckle. "He's actually being good for a change."

"I'm always good," retorted the sturdy eight-year-old boy. "An' she doesn't boss me around the way you do."

"Papa's home!" cried little Pauli as the door opened and a slender, neatly dressed man of average height came in. I thought he looked tired when Josephine introduced me, but he greeted me with a smile, and a few minutes later he was marching around the room with the baby on his shoulders.

"He has to do that every night," Mrs. Nicolini said, shaking her head, "or else Silvio cries. Come, come now. It's time to eat."

As Josephine had predicted, the food was plentiful: bowls of thick soup with which the meal began were followed by heaping plates of spaghetti smothered in the best tomato meat sauce I have ever tasted. This last was accompanied by thick slices of fresh Italian bread, and the dinner concluded with dishes of pistachio ice cream, in honor of the saint whose day we were celebrating.

I was putting on my hat and coat to go back to Bleecker Street when Tony said he needed a breath of air, and asked if I would mind if he walked me back to my place. Thank goodness he did; I was not at all sure of the route.

"Josie said you were thinking of going into the Navy," I said after we started out.

"Yes, I am. Office work is all right, I guess," he answered, "but working for an insurance company is dull, dull, dull, particularly the stuff they give me to do. I need to get out. I've put in my application—the family doesn't know about that yet—and if they take me, I'll be off like a shot. Mama won't like it, but Papa will understand. He knows what it's like to sit at a desk all day."

"I'm sure he does," I agreed, remembering the weary expression in the eyes of the senior Nicolini when he entered the house. "And as for your mother, Tony, you can't always do things her way. It's your life." What would his reaction be, I wondered, if he knew the lengths to which I had gone to avoid my mother's plans for me? "I'm sure the Navy will take you," I continued, glancing at his tall, broad-shouldered figure as we paused at a corner to let a cab go by. "And when your mother sees you in uniform, she'll be bursting with pride."

He smiled at that, and took my arm as we hurried across the cobblestones. I liked him, and enjoyed the walk, although I would have enjoyed it more if I hadn't had to be so guarded in the replies I made, or rather the lies I told about my upbringing. I had a feeling that Tony Nicolini was not a man who would countenance deceit. He held on to my arm for the rest of the walk, relinquishing it only at the foot of Mrs. Erdmann's stoop, where he waited until I waved to him through the glass panel in the front door.

"You sure made a good impression on my family, Mary Wick," Josephine said as she sat down at her machine Saturday morning. "They all liked you, 'specially Tony. He asked me if I thought you would go out with him some night, to an ice cream parlor or someplace. Do you think you would?"

She looked at me so hopefully, almost pleadingly, that I smiled and nodded just as the loud whirring of dozens of sewing machines started up. It would be something to do, I thought, as I ran off one long seam after another, someone to talk to of an evening.

Tony had more than a trip to an ice cream parlor in mind, though; when I returned home from work the next Tuesday, Mrs. Erdmann handed me a letter from him, the only mail I had received since taking up residence with her. It was an invitation to dine with him at Dinardi's restaurant on Friday, March 24, saying he'd be happy to pick me up at my address at seven o'clock.

"It's a swell place, Mary," Josie said when I told her I would like to go, and gave her a note for Tony. How different that little letter of acceptance was from the formal ones I used to write on heavy, monogrammed stationery! I had simply bought the cheapest pad of plain white paper I could find (five cents), two plain envelopes (two cents each), a bottle of ink (ten cents), and a straight pen (five cents), and written my short note. Then I filled in the rest of the evening by writing a longer letter to Rose in the little town of Broadville.

While I was pinning up my hair on Friday evening I thought longingly of my velvet wrap; it would have been just the thing for dinner at a "swell" restaurant, but as far as I knew, it was still up at the Foundling Hospital. Sister Mary Vee's plain black coat would have to do. The serviceable clothing she had packed for me was anything but dressy, and I'd had neither the time nor the money to spend on something new to wear. I had to be content with pinning a small bunch of artificial violets to the neckband of my one good shirtwaist. The milliner down the street had let me have them for ten cents.

"They're almost the same color as your eyes," Tony said when we were seated at a corner table in the crowded restaurant. "Ah, here are the menus. See anything you'd like to eat?"

"You'd better tell me what these Italian names mean, Tony. What is gnocchi?"

He explained, and ordered a series of dishes, all delicious, but I've forgotten the names of most of them except the antipasto, and the biscuit tortoni we had for dessert. I've also forgotten the greater part of our conversation; probably what happened the next day blotted it out from my mind. I do remember that it was all very pleasant, though, and that I willingly lingered over a glass of red wine while he talked about his dreams of seeing foreign lands.

"Palm trees, Mary, desert sands, islands baking in the sun, and no insurance companies, no snow!"

"Ah, but what would you do there, Tony?"

"Oh, I wouldn't live there. I just want to see it, see it all."

I realize now that Tony's desire to travel, his yearning for the tropics, was no more than a young man's quest for adventure before settling down, a substitute, in a way, for the grand tour of the well-to-do youths I had known. At the time, however, possibly because of my Palm Beach experience, I merely thought him incredibly immature.

"It's been a perfectly delightful evening, Tony," I said a few minutes later, "but I really must go now. Saturday is just another work day for me, you know."

I didn't tell him that I planned to make it my last work day at Triangle.

Once back in my room I took stock of my financial situation. I had managed to save a few dollars out of each week's pay, and with what I had left of Father's money I felt that I had enough to last for a fortnight while I looked for another position.

"I won't tell Josie until closing time," I thought as I climbed into bed. "That way she won't have time to try to persuade me to stay."

Unmistakable signs of spring were in the air on the morning of March 25, causing me to pause for a few minutes in Washington Square before crossing over to Greene Street and the dreary Ashe Building. I looked around at the houses that surrounded the park, wondering which one was Jerome's, but I knew that even if I could identify it, I wouldn't go near it. I was still too afraid.

I felt a bit like a traitor when Mr. Harris, one of the owners of Triangle, met me on the elevator and said I looked like Miss Springtime herself, but I managed to murmur a thank-you before we reached the tenth floor and he turned to the left to his office, while I went down the narrow hall to the right.

Everyone seemed unusually cheerful that day; maybe it was the weather, or perhaps just because it was Saturday. I felt almost buoyant myself, and when the closing bell rang at four forty-five, I stayed at my machine to finish the last seam in the last bodice top in the pile that had been handed to me that morning. I could have left it, and probably would have if I had been returning on Monday. Josie called to me that she'd be in the dressing room putting on her new spring hat, and would meet me at the elevator. Roberto was going to take her to look at bedroom furniture that evening.

At first I couldn't imagine why everyone was running past my machine in such a hurry, and then I heard the screams and saw the smoke billowing past the windows. The rest was sheer terror; suddenly I was caught up in the midst of a throng of girls, fifty or more, crowding into the narrow hallway, stumbling toward the elevator. When we passed the cutting room I saw flames shooting up from the bins that were placed under the tables to hold the "cutaways," or scraps of material too small to be of use. Those girls nearest the elevator pounded on the closed door, and when at last it opened they scrambled, tumbled, or fought their way in. One girl was half in and half out when the door began to close, and stayed there until those inside pushed her back into the hall.

When the smoke became denser, some girls ran through the flames to the windows; some jumped, I heard, but I didn't see that. One frantic group ran to the stairway and tried to push that door open, and others ran up and down the hall screaming for help. One girl's dress caught fire, and when she rolled on the floor to try to extinguish the flames, the others simply gave her as wide a berth as possible.

"The windows! The windows!" someone shouted, and I saw two more girls, one with her hair on fire, climb up on the windowsills. All at once a man—I don't know who he was—took charge. He shouldered his way through the screaming crowd still trying frantically to push open the staircase door. He forced the girls aside, and with a tremendous effort *pulled* the door open.

"Up, girls, up to the roof!" he shouted. "The way down is blocked. Up, up!"

We didn't have to be told twice. We crowded onto the staircase, coughing and sputtering from the smoke as we moved slowly upward. Halfway between the tenth floor and the roof, flames shot through a window that opened onto an airshaft, scorching our clothes, our hair, everything. Miraculously we got past it and staggered out onto the roof, an island in a sea of flames and smoke. Hell must look like this, I thought hysterically. Perhaps that's where I am.

Later, much later, I learned that some of us, myself included, had the New York University Law School to thank for our deliverance. I remember being on the roof, almost paralyzed with fear, when I heard men's voices urging us to hurry over to the ladders. We moved like a flock of sheep in the direction from which the voices came—we couldn't see very well through the smoke—and I remember that my arm hurt so badly that I could hardly climb the ladder to the top of the elevator shaft, an enclosure that rose twelve or fifteen feet above the roof. Then there was another ladder, but I had no idea where it went until Mark Delaney came to see me in the hospital carrying a bunch of lilies of the valley.

When I asked one of the tired, overworked nurses in the crowded charity ward of St. Vincent's Hospital when and how I had arrived there, she said that the fire had taken place two days earlier, but that she had no recollection of my being brought in.

"Some of you came in the ambulances," she said. "Some were carried in, and some walked in on their own, and we were workin' night and day takin' care of all the burns. Never mind how you got here, honey, just be glad you did, and that it's just your arm and some of your hair, not your pretty face that got burned."

She hurried off to tend to a patient who was moaning in a nearby bed, leaving me to wonder what I really looked like. My hair smelled terrible, and my right arm felt stiff, but otherwise I seemed to be unhurt. The woman in the bed on my right was so heavily bandaged that I could see only her eyes and mouth, and on my left, Gladys Monks, a girl who had had a machine near mine, lay crying softly.

"Gladys, don't cry," I said in a low voice. "You'll be all right."

"It's not me," she said tearfully, "it's my sister; I seen her jump out of the winder."

"Maybe someone caught her," I said. "Firemen have nets, you know. Did you see Josephine? I know she went to the dressing room when the bell rang."

Just then a young intern, holding what looked like a list of names in his hand, stopped next to my bed. "It says here that you have no relatives, Miss Wick. Is that right? No one we can notify? Someone to whom you can go when we discharge you? You can't stay here much longer, you know." He waited, pencil poised, for my reply.

"No," I answered. "There's no one, but I'll be all right. I have a room on Bleecker Street where I can stay until I'm ready to work again."

I thought he looked at me doubtfully, but after a moment he sighed and went on to question Gladys.

"I'm no hairdresser, honey," Nurse Jackson said after she'd helped me wash my hair the next morning, "but if you trust me, I can cut off the singed parts while your hair is still wet, and then you won't smell so bad."

Thank goodness the smell was gone when Mark came in during visiting hours that afternoon. I saw him, a tall, nice-looking young man with the broad shoulders of an athlete, walk slowly down the aisle between the beds, frowning slightly as he looked at each occupant.

"Do you recognize anyone?" I heard the nurse who was with him ask.

"Not yet," he said, shifting a bouquet of flowers from one hand to the other. "Oh, wait a minute! Yes, there she is!"

With that he hurried to my bedside and held out the flowers to me with a smile.

"This young man says he's the one who brought you in, Mary," the nurse said, "and see what he's brought to cheer you up! I'll put them in water for you. Ah, lily of the valley, my favorite."

"Did you—how did you—who are you? Oh, I mean thank you—" I knew I was gabbling, but he didn't seem to mind.

"No thanks, please. I don't really deserve them. I'm Mark Delaney, and I just happened to be handy when you were overcome, from the smoke, most likely."

"But where did you come from? How did you get me off that roof? I know I climbed a ladder, but that's all I remember."

He'd been attending a lecture, he said, a lecture given by a Professor Sommer on the tenth floor of the New York University Law School building, when the students heard the fire sirens. Some of the windows of the lecture hall overlooked the back courtyard, and they could see that the Ashe Building was on fire. They knew they had to help, and quickly made use of two ladders some painters had left on the roof of their own building. They used one as a bridge to the top of the elevator shaft, and lowered the other one to the roof of the burning building for the girls stranded there.

"You had climbed the permanent ladder leading up to the top of the shaft, and I guided you across the one to the Law School building. You were in a daze, but you did what I said, and when I got you into the lecture hall, you passed out cold. By the time I carried you downstairs, all the ambulances had either gone or were all filled up, but a fellow with a horse and wagon tossed all his crates out on the street to make room for us and some others. I can't say you arrived here in style, but arrive you did—and you look a hundred times better than when I left you here. What is your name, by the way?"

"Mary Wick. And I am deeply in your debt, Mark Delaney," I said, reaching for his hand. "How on earth can I repay you?"

He held my hand in both of his until I withdrew it. "Just give me permission to call on you, Mary Wick," he said with a smile, "and get better quickly."

Visiting hours were over a few minutes later, but before Mark left I learned that he was a lawyer, a junior partner in the firm of Osgood, Crale, and Mintner, of whom I'd heard my father speak. He had had an appointment with Professor Sommer in connection with a case he was working on, and had arrived before the lecture was over.

"I was early," he said. "Wasn't that fortunate? So I sat in on the end of the class to wait for him. We intended to retire to the bar of the Brevoort Hotel afterward to go over my case there, but—well, you know the rest. Look, I better run now, or the nurse will chase me. I'll be back tomorrow if I can get away from the office."

He came again two days later, this time with violets and a box of Park & Tilford's chocolates. He was anxious to know where I lived, and much as I liked what I had seen of him, and grateful as I was to him for saving my life, I wasn't sure that I wanted to go on seeing him. In the end, though, I gave him the address on Bleecker Street, saying that I'd be there until I was ready to start working again. I figured that I could always be "out" if he came, unless in the meantime I changed my mind about seeing him.

I wasn't sure when I would be discharged from the hospital, but as soon as Mark left that day, I began to make plans. It was the bunch of violets, now that I think of it, that reminded me of the conservatory in the Fifth Avenue house—and my parents were in Palm Beach . . .

On Saturday, April 1, exactly one week after the disaster on Greene Street, I went back to my rooming house dressed in an impossible shirtwaist that I couldn't wait to discard—my own had been in rags, they said—and my filthy, stained, bedraggled "other" skirt, with the money miraculously still safe in the waistband. I changed into fresh clothes, and after leaving a note and two dollars for Mrs. Erdmann, I took a cab up to Sixty-first Street. My plan was to collect a few articles of clothing and whatever else I thought might be of use to me. But first I would have to get past Collins.

Let him wire my parents, I thought. I'll be back on Bleecker Street before they get the telegram, and they'll never find me. But still I was nervous.

To my great relief it was Mollie, the kitchen maid, who opened the door for me.

"Miss Maida! Miss Maida, dear! Come in, come in! Mrs. Groome, come see! It's Miss Maida home again!"

In no time at all I was seated in my old place at the end of the kitchen table with a cup of strong tea and a plate of cookies in front of me while those two dear women hovered over me. Strangely enough, I was completely comfortable in the room where Ormley had lain bleeding on the floor. It was almost as if the kitchen knew he'd had no right to be there, and had expunged all memory of his presence.

I needn't have worried about Collins; he'd been taken to Palm Beach to help my father, who had sprained his ankle sometime in March.

"And then the mistress decided to take Lisette to look after her," Mrs. Groome said. "They was both that upset—the viscount's accident, you know."

"Were they worried about me?" I asked.

"Oh, mercy no. They knew you was havin' a grand time of it, seein' the sights of Europe with Lady Scale. Is that the latest hairstyle in Europe? Short like that?"

Without waiting for a reply, she hurried on. "But I think they missed you, and they was all upset when they heard that Mr. Jerome was plannin' to live in Italy for a while. He came home with his bride and collected the baby Christina, and off they went again. But he'll be back; he didn't sell his house. But oh, my gracious, it's mighty glad to see you we are, aren't we, Mollie?"

So that's what they gave out, I thought. How like Mother to come up with something elegant like a visit to my titled sister!

"And where is Emma?" I asked after a moment, wondering where the parlormaid was. "Did she go to Palm Beach, too?"

"Bless you, no," Mrs. Groome answered. "No need for a parlormaid there, any more than there is here in an empty house. No, your ma gave her a vacation till they come back the first of May, and she's gone to be with her mother and sister over in Brooklyn. So it's just Mollie and me, Miss Maida, and we'll take good care of you, that we will."

I knew they would, and I think it was partly that I didn't want to disappoint them that I changed my plans. Later that afternoon, while I was lingering in a deep, warm bath—being careful to keep my burned arm out of the water—the prospect of a month of luxury became too inviting to be easily dismissed. I could, I reasoned, just as readily look for a position from Fifth Avenue as from Bleecker Street, and wearing much better clothes than the few that hung in Mrs. Erdmann's closet.

The next morning, after sleeping soundly between my monogrammed sheets and eating a wonderful breakfast consisting of fresh orange juice, French toast, crisp bacon, and coffee, I dressed carefully and set out to find a hairdresser. I didn't dare go to Pierre, our regular man, but hunted around until I found a small salon over on Lexington Avenue. When I said that I'd been in the hospital with a high fever, and that they had cut my hair badly, the young woman assigned to me merely nodded and set to work. Because the singed ends had been cut off (although none too evenly), there was no need to mention the fire.

"You have lovely hair, miss," the operator said, handing

me a mirror as she stood back to admire her handiwork. "Let it grow for a few weeks, and then come back and let me shape it again for you."

I was glad she charged only fifty cents; my funds were running low, and I had yet to find a way of replenishing them. On my way home I stopped and bought a newspaper, intending to look over some of the advertisements for Help Wanted, but as I turned the corner of Madison Avenue and Sixtieth Street, I saw a sign indicating that an employment agency occupied the third floor of a brownstone house. When I saw the small hand-printed notice announcing an opening for someone with a knowledge of German, I climbed the stairs and knocked on the door of what I am sure had once been a hall bedroom.

"How good is your German?" the thin-faced woman behind the desk asked after she had read the application I filled out. "Are you fluent? I see you have not had much experience."

After I assured her that I could speak, read, and write German with ease, she looked me over thoughtfully for a moment before excusing herself and disappearing through a door into an adjacent room. A few minutes later she returned with an older man who asked me if I could read German script.

"Yes," I replied, "and I can write it, too."

He frowned as he studied me intently for a few moments, and then as he turned away I heard him say impatiently, "Oh, might as well send her along. We have no one else."

"Go up to this address," the woman said, handing me a slip of paper, "and ask for Mr. Augustus Schilling. He wants help with some German translations. And whether he hires you or not, report back to us."

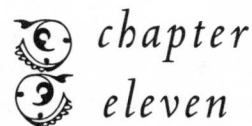

chapter
eleven

The butler who opened the door to the brick-and-limestone town house on Seventy-fourth Street just off Park Avenue could have passed for an older version of Collins—until he smiled. I don't believe I ever saw Collins smile.

"Miss Wick?" he asked. "The agency phoned, and Mr. Schilling is expecting you.

At first I thought the cheerful, sunlit library at the rear of the first floor was unoccupied, but when the butler announced me, a short, stout gentleman wearing striped trousers and a velvet smoking jacket popped up out of a wing chair that faced the windows. His rimless glasses had slid down almost to the end of his nose, and a pair of lively blue eyes looked out over them. Mr. Pickwick come to life, I thought.

"Ah, Miss Wick," he said in a high, almost childlike voice, "how do you do? Do you really know German? I do, a bit. Some of the very long sentences defeat me, though, and the fellow I had from Columbia couldn't do 'em either. But he was only a second-year student. Poor boy, he tried—but tell me, where did you study? Abroad?"

"No, my grandmother was German, Mr. Schilling. She

never spoke to me in English, and saw to it that I read the German poets . . ." I stopped, wondering how many more lies I would have to tell.

"Ah, then you will be able to do the work!" he exclaimed. "Now let me show you. You see, my grandfather spent his younger years in Germany, and after he made his fortune—inventions, you know—he came here with his wife and son—that was my father, you know—and made another fortune. Later on he devoted his days, sometimes nights, too, to writing a life of Friedrich der Grosse, Fred the Great, I call him. And when he tired of that, he'd write another chapter or two of a novel about castles and knights and maidens in distress. *Das Alte Schloss, The Old Castle,* is the name of it. Sounds like a good story, from what I can make out."

"And you would like them both translated?" I asked when he paused for breath.

"Exactly," he said, beaming at me as if I'd asked a brilliant question. "I'd like to know how the novel turns out; seems as if the heroine is in a peck of trouble. But the history of Fred the Great is the important work. So, here's my plan: we do ten pages of that, and then we do ten pages of *The Old Castle* as a reward! How does that strike you?"

Before I could reply, he had hurried over to one of the two desks against the wall and taken a sheaf of papers from a large cardboard box.

"Here is Chapter One," he said, thrusting a page at me. "Can you make any sense out of it?"

When I saw that the writing was in German script, I mentally thanked Fräulein Helff for insisting that I learn to read German handwriting, with all the *s*'s looking like *f*'s and all the *i*'s like *e*'s, and the *m*'s and *n*'s looking like each other.

"Frederick the Great, King of Prussia," I read aloud, "was born on January 24, 1712. His father wanted him to be a soldier, but to his sorrow his son became a scholar."

"That's fine, oh my, yes, that's very fine indeed! Yes, Miss

Wick, you'll do nicely. Now about your fee; will twenty-five a week be satisfactory? Good! Can you start tomorrow? Come every morning from nine to twelve; I go out in the afternoon, ride in the park, look in at my club . . ."

Mollie and Mrs. Groome showed no surprise at lunch, which I ate in the kitchen with them, when I said that I had more errands to do that afternoon.

"Yes, you'll be wantin' some clothes, no doubt," Mollie said, "seein' that yer trunk is so late comin' from Europe."

"Yes," I said, momentarily startled. "I don't know what can be causing the delay."

Were they beginning to wonder whether I'd really gone abroad? Would I have to make up some story and swear them to secrecy about my presence in the house? Not immediately, anyway. I needed time to dream up some more lies.

I went back to the employment agency, where the thin-faced woman told me that Mr. Schilling had paid my fee, and that I was a most fortunate young lady. I agreed; twenty-five dollars a week for three hours of work each day seemed like a fortune after the meager wages Triangle had paid. From there I went on to the rooming house to collect the few things I'd left there, and to let Mrs. Erdmann know I would no longer be needing the room.

I found two messages from Mark Delaney, asking me to write to him at the address he'd left, and one from Tony Nicolini saying he had been accepted in the Navy. I'll write to Mark, I decided, but not until after the first of May, when I'm settled at a new address. On twenty-five dollars a week I could afford a step up from Bleecker Street. But should I get in touch with him? Would it be fair to let him become seriously interested in me when I am not who he thinks I am?

Perhaps you will think I had become used to the idea of being a fugitive, or that I had come to believe that endangering a man's life, as I had done, was as inconsequential as swatting a fly. You would be wrong. I suffered miserably, not during the daylight hours when getting on in life as Mary Wick, worrying about money, and figuring out ways of avoiding identification as Maida Jardine occupied my mind—but oh! the nights! That is when the weight of guilt troubled me, and had ever since I'd seen the headline in the newspaper. Before that, I'd given scant thought to Ormley, but since then, I often had trouble banishing the picture of the viscount falling to the kitchen floor from my mind when I was trying to settle down to sleep. Some nights were full of horrible dreams in which I was pursued by people I didn't even know, and I would wake up bathed in perspiration, gasping for breath.

One night in the hospital I'd dreamed I was inside a ring of fire, and when I tried to call out for someone to help me, Ormley came walking through the flames, dressed all in black, and looking like the pictures of Mephistopheles in Fräulein Helff's worn copy of Goethe's *Faust*. When I woke up, a nurse was shaking me, saying I was having a nightmare and disturbing the whole ward.

It's the price I have to pay, I thought as I walked slowly through Washington Square Park, carrying my satchel and Aunt Eulalia's handbag. It occurred to me then that I might have to spend the rest of my life, fifty years or so, avoiding all the people who had known me in the past, and using a false identity with new acquaintances. I couldn't even risk returning the satchel and coat to Sister Mary Vee; she knew how I had fled from the kitchen after wounding Ormley, and would probably feel obligated to report me to the police since I was wanted, or had been wanted, for questioning.

None of it is my fault, I thought angrily. Mother caused the whole thing, and if Father hadn't made me run away that night . . . they're both to blame. Oh, *what* am I going to do?

Close to despair, I sat down on one of the park benches for a few minutes, and then, feeling calmer but having decided nothing, went on to Fifth Avenue to catch the uptown stage.

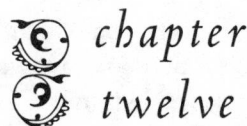

chapter twelve

Mrs. Groome and Mollie would have been shocked had they known I had taken a paying job—that simply was not done by girls in the Jardine family—but no eyebrows were raised when I left every morning for what they thought was instruction in the appreciation of painting and sculpture at the Metropolitan Museum. I stopped in at the museum on my way home from Mr. Schilling's one day and picked up little leaflets with pictures of statues and landscapes to show them.

How to break it to them that I would soon be moving out? I put it off until the last week in April, when it took me the better part of a rainy evening to convince them that I was not out of my mind and, more important, that I needed their cooperation in an innocent deception (if there is such a thing).

"I cannot tell you why I am going, Mollie," I said patiently. "You will simply have to believe me that I have a good reason for what I am doing."

"But Miss Maida," Mrs. Groome protested tearfully, "this is your home—"

"I know that, Mrs. Groome, but I must go. Now look, all I am asking of you is that you *never* say a word about my having been here, not to *anyone*. I am not asking you to tell any lies."

"But why?" Mollie asked again.

"I said I can't tell you, Mollie. Please don't ask me again. Someday you'll understand. I can trust you, can't I? I always could when I was a little girl."

"But how will you live? You'll be all alone." Mollie was almost crying.

"I'll manage. Don't worry. And I won't be alone—"

"Ah, it's elopin' you're up to, is it?" Mrs. Groome's eyes began to sparkle at the thought of a romance.

I made no answer to that, and they took my slight smile for acknowledgment. I did not disillusion them.

"Not a word from either of us, Miss Maida," the cook said cheerfully, getting up from the table. "He's a good feller, is he?"

"Ah, the best is none too good for you, Miss Maida," Mollie cried, almost smothering me with a hug. "And someday you'll be bringin' him to see us, will you not? But 'tis too bad we'll not be seein' you come down the aisle."

It was easier than I thought it would be, and the next day when I went off in a cab with two suitcases and Sister Mary Vee's satchel (Aunt Eulalia's handbag I left in its old place on the shelf of my closet), they waved me off, two unlikely conspirators, smiling happily at the thought of assisting in an affair of the heart.

Instead of going off to meet a lover, however, I settled in alone at Albion House, a small residential hotel which advertised "clean rooms for single gentlewomen at a modest stipend." The address on Forty-eighth Street near Third Avenue suited me; it was not in a neighborhood apt to attract any of the upper class, so I had no fear of running into any former acquaintances, either on the street or in the small dining room on the ground floor. After a bad moment one day when I was returning from Mr. Schilling's and caught sight of my sister Alicia crossing Park Avenue, I knew I couldn't be too careful.

I wasn't sure how long I could afford to live in Albion House; the room rent was ten dollars a week, which would leave me fifteen for everything else, but only for as long as it took me to get through *Fred the Great* and *The Old Castle*.

I enjoyed my mornings in that pleasant library, working steadily from nine to twelve, pausing only at ten-thirty, when Oliver, the butler, appeared with a tray of coffee and cookies. Mr. Schilling and I would chat during these intermissions, and it was during one of them that I told him I was puzzled by the pristine quality of the paper on which *Fred the Great* was written.

"Did they make this kind of paper in your grandfather's day, Mr. Schilling?" I asked. "It looks just like something I might buy in any stationer's today."

"Oh, bless me, no, no, no. Grandfather's manuscript is locked away. We are working from copies I had made. The originals are far too valuable and fragile—belong under glass in a museum. No, no, I had the copies made the last time I was in Heidelberg by a fellow who was a meticulous copier, but no good at translation."

"Did he copy *The Old Castle,* too? The handwriting looks the same."

"Yes, indeed. Did both. Took his time about it, too."

I wondered just how valuable the originals could be. The *Life of Frederick the Great* struck me as being incredibly dull and not very well written, but who was I to voice a critical opinion?

By the end of my first month with Mr. Schilling I had saved forty dollars, and I still had fifty-five dollars left of Father's money—I called that my "old money." I also had about fourteen dollars that I'd saved from my wages at Triangle. I knew I could manage for as long as Mr. Schilling employed me, and I was not unduly worried about what would happen next. I realized that I'd been extremely fortunate in finding such an agreeable, well-paying job with so little effort, but I was still immature enough to see no reason why something equally good should not come my way again.

The translations progressed steadily: *Fred the Great* was rather a bore at times, but *The Old Castle,* with its ramparts and dungeons, knights and ladies, romance and terror was more fun, a reward, as Mr. Schilling had said. He sat at the larger of the two desks in the library reading the morning paper, which he put aside when I placed a page of translation at his elbow. He never questioned my interpretation of his grandfather's prose; on the contrary, his remarks were invariably flattering.

"What a skill is yours, Miss Wick!" he would say. "Just look at the length of this German sentence! Remarkable! Remarkable! I marvel at how you can do it."

As soon as the the clock on the mantelpiece sounded the first stroke of noon, he'd jump up like a jack-in-the-box, exclaiming:

"Twelve o'clock and all's well! Put down your pen, Miss Wick; time to put work aside and get out in the fresh air." And he would ring for Oliver to show me out. No one could ask for a more considerate employer.

At first I did not mind the solitary life I had chosen for myself at Albion House, but by the end of my second week there I craved human companionship. None of the women I'd seen in the parlor or dining room seemed interested in making my acquaintance (just as well, I told myself; it would only mean more lies, and I had enough trouble keeping track of the ones I'd already told), and of course I dared not renew old acquaintances. I would have loved to have spent my afternoons at the Foundling Hospital with Sister Agnes and the babies, but that was out of the question.

When I left Mr. Schilling's house on Seventy-fourth Street, I generally walked over to Third Avenue, and then down Third to Forty-eighth, since there was little likelihood that I would run into Alicia or any of her friends that far east of Fifth Avenue. Most of them had probably left the city for their summer places, anyway. There were any number of small restaurants along my route, and one day in mid-June I stopped at a little Italian place for lunch. The food was inexpensive, and the tomato sauce, which was delicious, reminded me of the dinner I'd had at Josephine Nicolini's house. Half an hour later I was on the Third Avenue El on my way downtown to Mulberry Street.

"Bless the saints and all the angels in heaven!" Mrs. Nicolini cried when she opened the door for me. "Josie, Josie, look who's here! Come in, come in! We didn't know what had happened to you! Thank God your beautiful face wasn't burned. Oh, sit, sit. Only Josie and the baby are here. The others are at school, and Tony's gone to the Navy, so we'll have it nice and quiet. Josie, come!"

I almost didn't recognize my old friend when she limped into the room; she'd been what my brothers used to call "pleasingly plump" when we were making shirtwaists, and now she looked almost painfully thin. She wore a flowered scarf wound like a turban over her hair, and her eyes looked unnaturally large in a face that was pale and drawn. Her voice, though, warm and enthusiastic, was unchanged.

"Oh, Mary, Mary, you're alive! I couldn't find out anything about you. Oh, you look good! Don't mind me; I look a fright, but I'm getting better. Tell me, tell me how it was with you."

She took both my hands in hers and led me over to the sofa.

"Yes, I'll tell you, but first you; I want to hear about you, Josie."

"Oh, it's like a bad dream, Mary, and I don't remember all of it. You know how it goes in dreams? Sometimes there are gaps. Well, anyway, I came out of the dressing room, and everything was smoke and fire. I could hardly breathe and ran to a window, and when I turned around I saw the elevator door was open and all the girls were fightin' to get into the car. I ran, and the elevator started to go down with the door still open, so I waited until the top of the car came level with the floor and then I jumped onto it, and held on to a rope for dear life.

"I must've broke my ankle when I jumped. Anyway, I went down with the elevator, but I don't know how they got me off the top of it; I must've fainted. And I guess I banged my head on something and cut it open, because they had to shave off most of my hair. It's comin' back in again, slowly. They said I had smoke poisoning, and bleedin' inside me, somethin' internal, and kept me in a special part of the hospital ever so long. They wouldn't let me eat for a while, just liquids. See how thin I got? I'm gettin' along fine now, though. Mama's feedin' me good. Now tell me about you."

I gave her a shortened version of my experience with the fire and my stay in the hospital, and watched her eyes light up when I described the job I had with Mr. Schilling.

"That's the kind of work you should be doin', Mary mia," she said, nodding her head approvingly as Mrs. Nicolini came in with a tray of coffee and cake. "Much better than sittin' behind a machine all day long. Here, have some of Mama's cake; you're pretty thin yourself.

"Did you know that the owner of the Ashe Building is in trouble with the law? They say that he didn't have the proper exits and all, and now the building codes will be changed so that people won't be jumpin' out of the windows."

We talked quietly and comfortably until the children came in from school, Camilla and Anna looking as fresh as the morning in their summer dresses, Luigi with his hair rumpled and his jacket awry, and young Pauli in tears because someone had torn the picture he drew in kindergarten. As the noise level rose in that small living room I thought Josephine began to look tired, and after promising to come back again, I took my leave. I'd been afraid to ask about Roberto, since she didn't mention him, but I was happy to see a small diamond glistening on her ring finger. At least she had someone who loved her, someone in whom she could confide.

I had no one, and felt more alone than ever as I made my way back to my empty room. The feeling persisted, and after dining by myself in a corner of the hotel's restaurant I was so desperate that I wrote a note to Mark Delaney at the address he had left with Mrs. Erdmann. I mailed it at the post box at the corner, and went to bed feeling better. I felt even better when he replied by return mail, inviting me to have dinner with him on Thursday.

That was the day Mr. Schilling astonished me by proposing that I spend the summer at his lodge in the Adirondacks so that we could go ahead with the translations.

"It would be quite proper, Miss Wick," he said quickly when he saw me hesitate. "My niece and her three children spend every summer with me at Camp Magua—remember *The Last of the Mohicans*? My grandfather built it, and went there in July and August for many years. Then my father inherited it, and now it's mine. It's quite a beautiful spot, really, right on Lake Tanemund. I think you would enjoy the splendor of the forest, the fresh air, and being away from the heat of the city. You would have your own cottage, and our schedule would be the same: we'd work from nine to twelve, and the rest of the day would be yours to spend as you chose."

I must have still looked doubtful, for he held up his hand as if to ward off a blow, and said hurriedly:

"No, no, don't give me your answer now. Take your time; think it over. We won't leave for another fortnight."

I didn't have to think it over for very long; by the time I had begun to dress for dinner with Mark that evening, I had made up my mind that it would be foolish not to accept Mr. Schilling's offer. The alternative would be to spend the hot months in the city, something I had never done, and most likely unemployed at that. Also, the camp in the Adirondacks had the added advantage of being far removed from Newport and Glen Cove, eliminating the possibility of my running into anyone I'd known formerly.

"I'll tell him tomorrow that I'll be happy to spend the summer at Camp Magua," I said to myself, smiling at the recollection of how careful he had been to assure me that his niece would be there. I couldn't imagine that proper Pickwickian (probably in a nightcap) opening my door in the middle of the night à la Arnold Iverson.

I finished dressing, and was adjusting the belt on my dark-blue georgette dinner dress (one of two I had brought from Fifth Avenue) when the buzzer over my door announced a visitor for me in the parlor. I drew the matching scarf around my shoulders and tried not to hurry down the stairs.

"You fascinate me, Mary Wick," Mark said toward the end of our dinner in a small French restaurant on Fifty-second Street. "You jump from slave labor in a shirtwaist factory to a scholastic undertaking in the library of a wealthy man with no apparent effort, and now you're going off to continue your translations in the wilderness. I don't know what to make of you."

"Don't try, Mark. I don't quite know what to make of myself. My life recently has consisted of a series of strange episodes, but I've been fortunate, and never more fortunate than when you found me on top of that elevator shaft. I *owe* my life to you—I can't possibly thank you enough."

"Yes, you can, just by letting me see you soon again," he said quietly, looking intently into my eyes. "You said it would be two weeks before you leave, and I want as much of that time as you will let me have."

* * *

I saw him seven times during that fortnight: once for a stroll in Central Park, followed by tea at the Waldorf; once for an evening at the theater; and the other five times for dinner. I knew I was running a slight risk of being recognized in one of the restaurants Mark chose—all very expensive—but decided to take the chance, hoping that "Society" was out of town. No one paid any attention to me until one evening near the end of our meal, when Reggie Gardner, a young man I'd met a few times during my "season," passed our table.

"Excuse me," he said, bowing politely to me, "but aren't you . . ."

I said nothing, and stared at him as coldly as I could.

"Oh, I guess not. Excuse me, please," he murmured and hurried on.

Mark, who had started to rise, resumed his seat and looked across the table at me.

"Guess he likes your looks, too," he said with a smile. It could have been worse; Reggie Gardner could have mentioned my name.

On our last night together, he took me to a restaurant that boasted a small orchestra and dance floor. He held me gently in his arms while we waltzed, not too close, but closer than was customary at the balls I had attended. Later, in the deserted lobby of Albion House when I started to say good night, he pulled me to him, and bending his head slowly, kissed me gently, then with more fervor.

"I think I fell in love with you, dirty face and all, on top of that elevator shaft," he said softly before releasing me. "Come back to me, my darling." Then he turned and went quickly out into the dark street.

I lay awake for a long time that night, unable to stop thinking about him, what he meant to me and, more important, what he might come to mean in the future. I had no reason to think he hadn't believed the story I told him, the same one I'd told Rose and the others about growing up with my grand-mother on Long Island, but I knew that sometime I would have to tell him the truth. What effect would that have, I wondered, on his feelings for me?

He'd been anxious to tell me about himself right from the beginning, to establish his credentials, I suppose. He talked readily about his childhood in Washington, D.C., where his parents still lived on Dupont Circle, his years at Princeton, and then at Harvard Law School, and finally about his position with Osgood, Crale, and Mintner, whose offices were in the Equitable Building on Lower Broadway.

"It's a good firm, Mary," he said enthusiastically, "con-servative, reputable, and sound financially. They work me pretty hard, but it will be worth it if I'm made a partner in the near future. Then I'll be able to afford a town house; right now I have a flat, one floor in a brownstone on Twenty-fourth Street, with a crazy violinist above me and a pair of maiden ladies on the floor below. They really make quite a twosome: the younger one is wispy and thin, and shrinks away if I so much as say good morning to her, and the older one, tall and formidable, carries an umbrella, rain or shine, clutched in her fist. She looks as if she's quite ready to strike someone over the head with it. I give her a wide berth. Now it's your turn; I know where you live now, but tell me, what was your childhood like?"

"Very proper, very safe, and on the whole happy, although not particularly exciting. I think it was typical of life on a re-spectable, old-fashioned, tree-lined street in a small town. But being brought up by a grandmother is not like living in a family with two parents. She loved me, though, and I had the best of everything until she became ill and the money ran out. She wor-ried terribly about what would become of me. Thank heavens she taught me to love the German language, and to read Ger-man script. Do you know, Mark, Mr. Schilling said the other day that the original of *Fred the Great* is too fragile to handle?

We're working from a copy he had made—of that and *The Old Castle*. He keeps the originals in a safe."

"Amazing, the things people treasure," Mark said with a slight shake of his head. "I have a client who has insured a moth-eaten old toupée she says is the one her great-uncle wore when he shook hands with Abraham Lincoln. She wants to leave it to the Metropolitan, and can't understand why they show so little interest in it. But tell me, is Schilling going to publish your translation?"

"He hasn't said. I can't imagine who'd read it if he did."

"History buffs, maybe. Schilling probably reasons that he's doing humanity a service, and in the meantime he has the pleasure of your company. Did your grandmother ever tell you that you would grow up to be a beautiful woman?"

"No, she did her best to discourage vanity, and to make me realize that good manners and sitting up straight were all-important."

All the lies I've told, I thought, turning over in bed and trying to settle down for the night. I can't go on telling them; it isn't fair to Mark, and I like him too much. Perhaps I'll write to him from Camp Magua and make a clean breast of the whole business. Then I'll feel better—but then I might never see him again. No, I can't tell him about Ormley; he's a lawyer, and would have to tell the police where to find me. I wonder, though: it's been four months since Valentine's Day, and I've seen nothing about either Delcannon or Ormley in the paper since March. Maybe Ormley has recovered, and the whole thing is forgotten. Perhaps Mark and I will have a good laugh about it someday.

Mr. Schilling was not one to willingly deprive himself of the good things of this world, his "creature comforts," as he called them, while purportedly roughing it in the wilderness. Oliver, the butler, along with a cook and two maids, had been dispatched to Camp Magua three days before Mr. Schilling and I left New York, in order to lay in supplies, air the rooms, and in general have everything ready for us. All four of them stood smiling on the porch steps as our horse-drawn station wagon drew up in front of the main lodge, a cheerful welcome after an uncomfortable trip over six miles of rutted dirt roads, along which I had seen no sign of human habitation.

"Peaceful, eh, Miss Wick?" Mr. Schilling asked as I stood looking out over the sunlit lake a short distance away. "There's Esmé, my niece, down there with her young ones. You've time to bathe before dinner, should you wish. Just follow that path to the right of the hemlocks. But perhaps you'd rather see your cabin first. Whatever you like. Dinner is at seven o'clock."

I liked what I saw: Camp Magua consisted of four cabins, a main lodge flanked by two guest cabins, plus a smaller one in the rear for the help, all surmounted by a common roof. I learned later there was a fifth cabin nearby, not visible from the lodge, inhabited year-round by one Joseph Higby, a shy, bearded giant who acted as caretaker-cum-handyman.

"Don't be afraid if you see him, Miss Wick," Oliver said. "He's big, but he's harmless, keeps to himself, a hermit, you might say."

My own quarters were more than adequate for my needs, with a built-in banquette for a bed in one corner, a rustic worktable under one of the shining six-paned windows, and three surprisingly comfortable wooden rocking chairs with seats of woven rushes grouped in front of a large stone fireplace. Red-and-yellow cretonne pull curtains, an oval-shaped braided rug, a sturdy dresser, and two oil lamps completed the furnishings. I opened a door to what I took for a second clothes closet, but which turned out to be a small bathroom containing a sink, toilet, and shower bath. "Water piped in from the lake," Mr. Schilling had said proudly, "no need to haul it ourselves." And no need for chamber pots or covered ways, I thought gratefully.

The next morning Mr. Schilling and I sat down to work at the long refectory table in the living room of the main lodge, and when Oliver came in as usual at ten-thirty with coffee and cookies, it occurred to me that my employer might not realize that he was not only paying me a salary, but also providing me with room and board. If he did, he said nothing about it, not even at the end of the first week, when he handed me twenty-five dollars in new bills.

"No place to spend it here, Miss Wick," he said with a chuckle, "unless you want to ride in to the general store in Broadville with Oliver someday. It's a bit closer than the station, but there's nothing much there."

"Broadville!" I exclaimed, remembering Rose Reiner. "I think I know someone who lives there, a girl I worked with last winter."

"Splendid! Go visit her some afternoon. I'll arrange it with Oliver. He goes in twice a week, sometimes three times. You could visit with your friend while he goes over to the station at Pinesbridge to pick up the mail."

I meant to take advantage of his offer, but as the days slipped by in lazy, pleasant monotony, I kept putting the excursion off. Actually, I had no strong desire to see Rose again; she belonged in the past, to an episode in my life that had not been particularly happy. So did Josie, but that was a different relationship. Another thing that influenced my decision not to look Rose up was pure selfishness: the weather throughout July was remarkably good, and the prospect of an afternoon spent bathing in the clear blue water of Lake Tanemund and relaxing afterward on its sun-drenched banks was far more enticing than a hot trip in that uncomfortable station wagon.

I'd learned to swim fairly well as a child, and when Esmé Allbright, Mr. Schilling's niece, asked me if I would help her oldest girl with the breast stroke, I said I would. I didn't quite know what to make of Esmé; her manner toward me was polite enough, but it could never have been called friendly. I suppose that since I was a paid employee—part of the hired help—I didn't qualify as a guest. The little girls, however, were engaging, and I enjoyed spending time in the water with them.

I really don't know what their mother had to be so snooty about; her husband, I gathered from remarks at the dinner table, was a hardworking and poorly paid banker in Albany, so intent on rising to the top of his profession that he wouldn't take a vacation. Unsure of himself, I thought. I wondered briefly what life was like in the Allbright household—Esmé certainly did not seem like a happy woman.

I also began to wonder what Mr. Schilling was looking for in the pages of *The Old Castle* that I translated. He wasn't just reading them now, he was scrutinizing them, going back over the earlier ones again and again. Several times I saw him shake his head as he read over what I wrote, and one morning I heard him mutter, "Not here, it's just not here." I hesitated to ask him what he meant until the afternoon I went back to the lodge to pick up a book I'd left there in the morning. I found him in his usual chair at the refectory table, poring over the completed pages of the biography, so engrossed that at first he didn't see me.

"It must be here someplace," he said, rubbing his eyes, "but where? We're three-quarters of the way through—ah, Miss Wick! I didn't know you were here."

"Were you looking for something special?" I asked. "Would you like me to go over some part—"

"No, no. I trust your translation, but . . . oh, well . . . you see, you see . . . oh, perhaps I had better tell you," he said haltingly. "You see, you see, I am looking for something."

I waited while he took a large white handkerchief from his pocket and patted his face delicately with it.

"You see, Miss Wick, there is a clue somewhere, and I think it is in this rather dull history of Fred the Great, yes, a clue."

"A clue to what, Mr. Schilling?"

"At least my dear father said there was. It seems that Grosspapa made a great to-do about how a careful reading of his writings would reveal the whereabouts of the Czarina's ruby, a great treasure worth a king's ransom. My father laughed when he told me the story, and said that that was the only way the old gentleman could get anyone to read his books. For years I believed that—you've seen how poor his writing is—but recently I began to take him seriously, and now I can't think of anything but the ruby. You might say I am obsessed with the mystery of this mighty gem—ah, Oliver, thank you."

The butler had come in quietly, and now he carefully placed a small silver tray containing a decanter of whiskey, a glass, and a carafe of water on the table.

"Ah, yes," Mr. Schilling said eagerly. "Time for a bit of something liquid. Miss Wick, will you join me?"

"Perhaps Miss Wick would prefer iced tea, sir," Oliver said softly.

"Thank you, I would, Oliver," I agreed, and we sat in silence until the iced tea appeared and the butler had withdrawn.

"Where was I? Oh, yes, the ruby." Mr. Schilling put his glass down, and clasping his hands together, leaned closer to me. "You see, Miss Wick, that's why I wanted someone like you to work for me, not some sharp professional translator who might stumble on the clue and make off with the ruby. I knew as soon as I saw you that you could be trusted with the crown jewels if they came your way. I am an excellent judge of character. But, my oh my, where is that clue? Certainly not in the section on the Seven Years' War."

"Do you think we should be looking for a reference to the ruby, or to the hiding place? Which?" I asked more out of politeness than from real interest.

"Either one, either one," he replied. "And now that you know what I'm after, so much the better. Maybe you'll spot something. Not a word to Esmé, mind you. She thinks I'm a bit flighty as it is. Not much sense, that one. I only put up with her for her mother's sake; I loved my sister dearly. But Oliver knows what I'm doing; he's a good fellow, Oliver, been with me for years. You can trust him."

I began to feel that I was becoming involved in a small, probably harmless, conspiracy, a feeling reinforced that evening after dinner when Oliver paid an unexpected visit to my cabin.

"Excuse me, Miss Wick," he said when I opened the door, "but I wanted a word with you, just to ask you to go along with Mr. Schilling, sort of humor him. It's all romantic nonsense about the ruby, of course, but the search keeps him happy. He takes these notions, you see. Once we were three years trying to raise the pure white peony someone offered a prize for, and every one that we got to bloom had a speck of red in the middle."

"Come in, Oliver, and sit down," I said, suddenly curious about my employer's past undertakings.

"Thank you, Miss Wick. And another time we went looking for sunken treasure, Spanish doubloons, off the coast of Mexico. He'd seen a picture of a wrecked ship in the newspaper, and nothing would do but that we go and see for ourselves. Divers brought up pieces of an old galleon, bits of waterlogged wreckage, is all. And now it's the Czarina's ruby; at least we're on dry land this time. He takes these notions, and no one can talk him out of them. He may be fifty years old, but he's still a boy at heart. Just humor him, Miss Wick; this, too, shall pass."

"Have you been with him long, Oliver?"

"Twenty years, Miss Wick. He's been very good to me. He found me lying in the street one night—some thugs had beaten me up—got me to a hospital, then took me into his home. At first I needed him, but now I think it's the other way around, and he needs me. He's a good, generous man, Miss Wick, and if at times he's a bit strange it doesn't matter. It's all harmless. And then of course . . ."

"Of course what, Oliver?" I asked gently when he hesitated.

"It's his health, Miss Wick," he said so softly that I had to lean forward to hear him. "He's had angina for some time now, but he won't admit it. Says it's just neuralgia or something, and although he heard what the doctor said, he pretends it's going away, that the medicine is curing it. Actually it's something for the pain that he's taking, nitroglycerine, the doctor said when he gave me instructions about the dosage and told me to make sure we always have it handy, because we'd never know when he'd need it. I don't know how much longer . . ." Oliver's voice broke slightly before it trailed off.

"Poor man," I said after a moment, "and poor you, Oliver. Mr. Schilling is lucky to have you to care for him, but that doesn't make things any easier for you. At least he doesn't sit around moaning and groaning about his condition—he's putting a brave face on it, isn't he?"

Oliver nodded, and we sat without speaking for a few minutes. Then, when he continued, I could hear genuine affection in his voice.

"Yes, he's a good man. I doubt that he ever did a day's work in his life; he didn't have to, with all that he inherited from his father and grandfather, but he gives a lot away, helps the needy, and what if he does go off on 'quests,' as he calls them? They keep him happy, and no one gets hurt. So play along, will you, Miss Wick?"

I promised I would, but after Oliver left and I sat thinking over what he had said, I wondered if Mr. Schilling might not be doomed to disappointment in his latest "quest." I wouldn't want to hurt his feelings, but would it not be kinder in the end to try to discourage him gently in what seemed to me (and to Oliver) a fruitless pursuit?

I have never, I am sure, spent as much time with my pen in hand as I did that summer. When the weather broke the first week in August and we had a succession of rainy, drizzly, or misty days, I suggested that we spend afternoons as well as mornings on the manuscripts, a proposal Mr. Schilling greeted with enthusiasm. In addition to all the writing that entailed, I had Mark's letters to answer. He wrote frequently, sometimes a short note from the office on legal paper, but more often a long letter on his personal stationery, probably written in the evening in his flat in the brownstone on Twenty-fourth Street. They were all love letters, the first I'd ever had, and I couldn't help reading and rereading them when I was alone in my cabin at night. I had Oliver buy me a box of writing paper and filled the flimsy sheets with accounts of life at Camp Magua and assurances to Mark that I missed him, but not that I loved him, although I was pretty sure that I did.

Esmé and the little girls were at loose ends during the rainy weather; she was bored and short-tempered, and the children were so cranky that even gentle, kind Mr. Schilling scolded them and finally banished them from the lodge. He and I, on the other hand, were quite content to spend the greater part of each day at the refectory table, which Oliver had moved over in front of the massive stone fireplace. We worked steadily, pausing only to drink the coffee or tea that the cook sent in at ten-thirty and again at three-thirty.

"Maybe the clue is in *The Old Castle,* Mr. Schilling," I said late one afternoon after struggling with a tiresome account of Fred the Great's troubles with Austria. "Perhaps we should concentrate on finishing that."

"What a splendid idea, Miss Wick! I need a bit of romance to cheer me up, even if it is rubbish. Where did we leave the beauteous Friedelinda last time? Was she still imprisoned by the Black Knight?"

By the end of the afternoon the maiden in distress had managed to escape from her dungeon with the help of her faithful maid, Elmidora, and was wandering through the dark forest hoping that her lover would find her.

"Well, of course he will," Mr. Schilling said, mildly exasperated. "And he'll wound the Black Knight in a fierce combat, carry Friedelinda off to his kingdom, and live happily with her forever after. What balderdash! Nothing there resembling a clue!"

"There are still about fifty pages left—" I began.

"Right you are, Miss Wick! Never despair, I say. There's bound to be a clue, and we'll find it!"

We did find it the following day, and I wish with all my heart that we hadn't.

chapter fourteen

In Chapter Thirty-nine of *The Old Castle* Friedelinda and her handsome husband (who turns out to be the Crown Prince Rudolf of Saxony) are made welcome at the court of Ivan the Terrible. The Czar, a man known for his appreciation of young beauty, is so enchanted with the charms of Friedelinda that he presents her with a valuable ruby that had been intended as a gift for his fifth wife. He would have welcomed our heroine in his bed, too, but since she is the sister of the powerful king of Poland, whose support Ivan needs in his efforts to conquer the Baltic states, he reluctantly refrains from having her brought to his chamber by his boyars.

"There it is, Miss Wick," Mr. Schilling all but shouted. "There's the ruby, the Czarina's ruby! Go on, go on! We're getting close!"

He leaned over my shoulder as I continued to write:

> After many banquets and entertainments given in their honor, Friedelinda and her prince left for home with their retinue of servants . . .

"No, no, don't write any more!" Mr. Schilling ordered. "Read it aloud to me. It will be quicker. You can write it later."

He listened intently to several pages devoted to the details of the couple's hazardous trip back to Saxony, a journey fraught with encounters with brigands, hampered by storms, bad roads, and occasional breakdowns of carriages. At last Rudolf and his bride are forced to take shelter in the cottage of a woodsman who welcomes them, but tells them that they may not be safe from the bands of robbers who inhabit the surrounding forest:

" 'I tell you this, my lord and lady,' the woodsman said, 'to warn you. Undoubtedly they have seen you, even though you have not seen them. They know how to make themselves invisible, and if they think—as is likely—that you carry riches with you, they will attack in the darkest hour of the night.'

" 'I shall be ready for them,' the prince said stoutly, drawing his sword from its sheath.

" 'They won't hurt you if you give them your gold and your lady's jewels—' the woodsman began.

" 'My jewels, my precious ruby!' cried Friedelinda.

" 'You must give them something,' continued their host.

" 'A few things will pacify them. But you must hide your most valuable ones. Here, I will show you.'

"He moved over to the hearth, and taking an iron tool from the mantel, loosened one of the large stones that made up the wall around the fireplace. A few moments later he lifted the heavy stone out, exposing a dark cavern the size of a man's head.

" 'Put your most precious gems here, my lady,' he said, 'and most of your gold, my lord. They will be safe behind the stone. When I replace it no one will know. You can trust me.' "

"Behind the stone, behind the stone!" Mr. Schilling shouted, jumping up and rushing over to his own fireplace. "That's the clue! That's it! But which stone? Which one? Come, Miss Wick, help me see which one is loose! Call Oliver!

He can help us. See if you can detect any sign, however small, that a stone has been moved!"

From then on there was no peace at Camp Magua. Mr. Schilling was excited enough when we began to examine the stones that surrounded the fireplace, but when they all proved to be as securely wedged in place as the stones of the Incas in their walls, he acted like one possessed.

"It's here, I know it's here," he said over and over again. "I'll find it if I have to . . ."

He did not complete that sentence, but when I met Oliver's eyes I knew that we had both come to the same conclusion. Mr. Schilling would not be satisfied until he found the ruby, even though it meant removing each and every stone in the place.

"Shouldn't we finish the novel, Mr. Schilling?" I asked when he flung himself down into a chair and sighed heavily.

"No point in that now," he said wearily. "We've found the clue. Who cares what happens to that silly girl? It's the ruby—"

"But sir, if I may be so bold," Oliver interrupted, "is it likely that such a jewel would have been in your grandfather's possession without anyone else's knowledge? It must be worth a fortune. Wouldn't he have—"

"How do I know what he'd do with it?" snapped Mr. Schilling. "I was only a child when he died. But it's as clear as this hand in front of my face that it's here. I know it's here, and I intend to have it. Then I, Augustus Reinhold Schilling, will be famous. I'll be known as the owner of the ruby of the Czarina!"

I could think of nothing to say to discourage him, and after murmuring that I felt tired, I slipped away.

August 15, 1911

Dear Mark,

Quite suddenly Camp Magua has changed from a peaceful retreat in the wilderness to a place filled with noise and confusion, in order to avoid which I have carried my writing materials down to the edge of the lake. Even here I can hear sounds from the lodge. You see, when Mr. S. decided that the clue we were looking for (I wrote to you about that) was in the words "behind the stone," he became convinced that the Czarina's ruby is concealed in the fireplace wall at the lodge.

He has Joseph Higby, the taciturn caretaker, removing the stones one by one, a difficult job, since some of them are enormously heavy. Fortunately, Higby is a powerful man, but I don't think he is happy with what he is doing. He looked quite angry yesterday when he dropped a stone close to his foot—that's when I decided to stay out of the way. In fact, I am thinking of leaving as soon as I conveniently can. Esmé Allbright packed up yesterday and took her children home to Albany; she said she thought her uncle had gone crazy.

Later: It's evening now, and I am in my cabin. I was interrupted this afternoon by screams from the cook and the maids. It seems that when Higby pried out a certain stone, six or seven others came crashing down, and they thought it was an earthquake.

Mark, I am really worried about Mr. S., and so is Oliver. He (Mr. S.) looks awful; he hasn't shaved in days, and won't go to bed at night. He just sits and stares at the wall. And his clothes are filthy. Maybe Esmé was right. I want to leave, but he's been so kind to me that I hate to desert him. We were supposed to return to the city the first week in September, but heaven only knows when we'll be going now.

I miss you,

Mary

When I gave Oliver my letter to mail the next morning, he told me he had finally persuaded Mr. Schilling to sleep in his bed the night before.

"I told him off, Miss Wick. I told him he was a disgrace to Camp Magua, that his father would have been ashamed of him, and that he had no right to act like a spoiled brat and upset everyone. And do you know, he took it from me. He even apologized."

"Is he having the stones put back?" I asked.

"Not yet, but he can't take any more out because Higby quit. Said he was a caretaker, not a stonemason. Mr. Schilling argued that it didn't take a mason to remove stones, but Higby walked out anyway."

After Oliver left I went into the lodge to see what Mr. Schilling proposed to do. He was sitting at the refectory table surrounded by stones, frowning as he smoothed out a piece of crumpled paper.

"I don't know what to make of this, Miss Wick," he said. "But I'm wondering if it could be another clue."

He sounded tired, all the earlier enthusiasm gone from his voice.

"It was stuck to one of the stones that fell in that heap over there," he continued. "It's in German, and rather faint writing. See what you can make of it, will you, please?"

The ink was indeed faded and it was only with difficulty that I could decipher the message.

"I can't be sure, Mr. Schilling," I said a little later, "but here is what I think it says: 'So, you found the words *behind the stone*, did you? And you thought that was the clue? And that you wouldn't have to finish the novel? Perhaps you had better read it to the end!' Yes, I'm pretty sure that's what it says."

"Where is *The Old Castle*, Miss Wick?" he asked crossly. "We'll finish it, damn it. We've gone this far—"

So once again we sat down with Friedelinda and Rudolf. I

read aloud while my employer sat perfectly still opposite me listening to the final adventures of the romantic pair.

"Two hours after midnight, a band of robbers broke into the cottage, but the valiant prince, true to his boast, slew two of them with his sword, and the rest fled in disarray without so much as a single gold coin. The precious ruby and other valuables were retrieved from their hiding place. Rudolf rewarded the woodsman handsomely for his hospitality, and as dawn was breaking, the royal couple resumed their journey through the vast forest."

"What kind of author is he?" Mr. Schilling asked petulantly. "He says nothing about the retinue of servants, or where they spent the night."

"Perhaps he forgot about them," I said, "or maybe—"

"Oh, well, go on, go on, Miss Wick."

"When Rudolf and Friedelinda arrived at the prince's ancient castle in Saxony, they learned that news of the Czar's gift had preceded them, and that a neighboring ruler, the king of Upper Nierstein, had taken a solemn vow that he would have the gem for his crown. 'He says the Czar promised to reward him with it for sending an army to his aid, and has not done so,' Rudolf's Lord Chamberlain reported. 'You must hide the stone, Your Highness. Even now the king's envoy is on his way here.' "

"Now read carefully, Miss Wick," Mr. Schilling interrupted, "because there's another hiding place coming, another clue. I can feel it."

Afraid that I would miss something of importance, I read slowly through four pages devoted to a frantic search for the perfect hiding place for the ruby. At last, at long last, I came to it: when the footsteps of the envoy were heard approaching the great hall of the castle, Friedelinda in desperation dropped the gem into a marble urn that contained a bouquet of spring flowers.

"Ah, the urn!" exclaimed Mr. Schilling. "I have a marble

urn! That must be it! The urn, Oliver! You know it! We'll return to New York at once. It's there!"

"You mean the urn in the library, sir? The one next to the bust of Socrates on the high shelf?" Oliver, who had been standing quietly in the doorway, looked dubious.

"Of course, of course; what other urn do we have?" Mr. Schilling demanded. "Pack up, Oliver. We'll leave first thing in the morning."

It all seemed rather childish to me; if, by some remote chance, the ruby was in the marble urn, how could it have escaped notice over the years? I remembered that on a few occasions when I had arrived at the Seventy-fourth Street house shortly before nine o'clock, I'd seen a housemaid leaving the library carrying her brooms and brushes with her. Wouldn't she, or someone, during the spring or fall cleaning, have removed the urn from the shelf, presumably to dust or wash it? Surely the ruby would have been discovered then, perhaps pocketed, and no one the wiser.

I felt far from sanguine concerning the success of our search as we made our way, hot and tired, through the Friday-afternoon crowds in Grand Central Station toward the line of cabs on Vanderbilt Avenue. Mr. Schilling and two porters hurried on ahead, and for a moment or two I lost sight of them, but Oliver, who saw me hesitate, nodded in the direction we were to take.

As I peered through the crowd I caught sight of a slender man dressed in a light fawn-colored suit, obviously bound for a weekend in the country. He turned at that moment to face us, and before I could lower my gaze I saw—no one could miss it—the ugly red scar that ran from his left eyebrow across his forehead and disappeared beneath the hat that was slightly tilted toward the back of his head. At that moment Mr. Schilling, out of breath and red-faced, appeared at my side, and as he took my arm and guided me through the crowd to the waiting cab, I felt as though Ormley's eyes were not only following me, but also piercing a hole in my thin summer dress and stabbing me between my shoulder blades.

I sighed with relief when we pulled up in front of the Schilling house. No one had followed us from Grand Central that I could see. The only other cab in sight was the one with most of the luggage and the maids. My mind, however, was not at rest. Ormley had recognized me, I knew that, and I also knew how bent on revenge he would be, revenge in the form of a forced marriage and a dowry of two million dollars.

At least I didn't cause his death, I thought, as we mounted the steps to the large front door; I may have disfigured him horribly, but I am not a murderess. I couldn't, however, take much consolation in the thought that Ormley was alive, and even less in the thought that he had recognized me. I would still have to hide, from him and from my mother.

I followed Oliver down the hall to the library, where Mr. Schilling was already tugging at the mahogany stepladder, trying to place it in front of the shelf from which Socrates looked down on us.

"That's it, Oliver, carefully, carefully, hand it down to us," he said as the butler reached for the urn.

"It's heavy, sir, mighty heavy," Oliver warned. "Better let me put it on the table for you."

From where I stood I could see that the mouth of the urn was less than two inches in diameter, far too small to allow a human hand to explore its depth, but before I could look around for a slender pair of tongs or some other instrument, Mr. Schilling had turned the urn upside down and was shaking it gently. Nothing happened, but when Oliver shook it more vigorously, a tightly folded piece of dusty paper bounced out onto the tooled-leather tabletop. With fingers that trembled, Mr. Schilling unfolded it and a moment later a small red stone lay in the palm of his hand.

"It's a garnet," he said in a hollow voice, "and not worth

much more than a piece of red glass. See if there's anything written on the paper, will you, Miss Wick?"

The message this time was as short and wickedly mischievous as the last one, and I felt unreasonably angry at the writer as I translated it aloud:

"Alas, no ruby, just a garnet that fell out of one of my wife's earrings. But it was a splendid story, and a royal treasure hunt, was it not?"

I slipped quietly out of the room, unwilling to witness what I knew would be all too apparent in the face of the child-man who had been so kind to me. I wanted a cab to take me down to Albion House, and looked out the window in the front parlor to see if one had waited. To my surprise one was parked on the opposite side of Seventy-fourth Street, and I was about to signal to the driver to come and take my suitcases when I caught a glimpse of a figure in a fawn-colored suit half-hidden in the areaway of the house across the street.

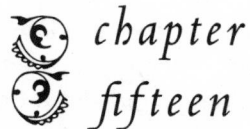

chapter
fifteen

"Is anything wrong, Miss Wick?" Oliver had come into the room so quietly that I hadn't heard him. "You look so white."

"I'm just terribly tired," I answered. "It's been a very long day."

"Indeed it has, Miss Wick. Come back into the library; I'm just getting some sherry and biscuits for Mr. Schilling, and I think a bit would do you good. Don't worry about him, miss. He'll get over it. He always does, and before you know it, he'll be off into something else with never another thought for the ruby."

"Well, he won't need me any longer, Oliver, unless whatever he does involves German. I really should be on my way. Would you mind if I used the telephone?"

It had occurred to me that if I could reach Mark, I could ask him to escort me back to Albion House, where I'd be safe for the night at least, but there was no answer either at his office or at the flat. Of course he couldn't have known . . .

As it was, I ended up spending the night in a charming guest room on the third floor of the Schilling house. Over the sherry and biscuits Mr. Schilling cheered up considerably, and by the time he finished his second glass he was chuckling.

"Imagine, Miss Wick, imagine the colossal nerve and grim determination of the old man! Look at the lengths he went merely to guarantee that someone, even just a member of the family, read the trash he wrote. He takes the cake for perseverance.

"I should have known better," he went on, leaning back comfortably in his armchair. "Trouble was, you see, I never really knew him. I've only the haziest recollection of a big man with a deep voice and a shock of white hair. Of course he was brilliant, had the mind of an inventor, but he certainly didn't invent a very good novel, did he? And as for Fred the Great— well, that's just a dull, boring list of facts."

I murmured my agreement, and after a moment or two asked him what he intended to do next.

"Don't know yet. Have to think about it. Can't sit idle and let the world go by, you know. My soul, is that thunder? Oh my, yes, and it's begun to rain. You can't go out in this, Miss Wick. You'd best stay the night. Oliver! Is the guest room in order? Miss Wick will be staying the night, will you not, my dear?"

My first thought upon awakening the next morning was that I would have to leave New York again, and my second one was that I was sick and tired of hiding, of running away. First the orphan train and Michigan, then the shirtwaist factory, and then the Adirondacks. Where next? Was I never to be allowed to settle down to some kind of proper life? Now Ormley had seen me and followed me, and it was just a matter of time until he confronted me. Then, suddenly, it occurred to me that now that I knew definitely that he was alive I could go home to Fifth Avenue or, at this season, to Glen Cove, and face up to my family, secure in the knowledge that I was not a murderess. Or I could go to Mark, tell him everything, and ask his advice.

Once he heard my story he'd understand why I hadn't been honest with him, wouldn't he? Or would he feel that he'd been duped?

"But you're not leaving for good, are you, Miss Wick?" Mr. Schilling asked plaintively at breakfast. "I thought perhaps you'd stay on, help out, you know."

He looked so troubled that I couldn't refuse him point-blank. "Well," I said slowly, "perhaps, Mr. Schilling, I could help out, but I'm not sure how. And right now I need some time—"

"Of course, of course you do!" he exclaimed. "What have I been thinking of? You've worked for months with never a day off. Take all the time you want, and then let me know when you're ready to return. You are a good companion, Miss Wick, and I shall miss you. But of course you must go for now. Oliver will call a cab for you."

I saw no sign of Ormley as I left Seventy-fourth Street, and on the way downtown I was so busy thinking about getting in touch with Mark that I didn't notice the black limousine that drew up behind my cab at Albion House. The doorman came out to take my suitcases, and I had started to follow him into the hotel when Ormley appeared at my side. He grasped my arm firmly, and when I turned sharply, trying to shake him off, I looked straight into the cold, angry eyes of my mother. Of course, I thought, in a lightning flash of understanding, he would have enlisted her help as soon as he spotted me. She turned away from me to instruct the doorman to place my suitcases in the trunk of the limousine, explaining that I was her daughter and she had come to take me home. He looked surprised, but he did as he was told.

"Get into the car, Maida," she commanded. "At once."

She took my other arm, and between them they forced me into the limousine, which I now recognized as my father's.

"Where . . . how . . ." I began as the chauffeur started the engine.

"You are in no position to ask questions, Maida," she said crossly. "And I am exhausted. So is the viscount. We've both been up half the night on your account. Now be quiet, and let me rest. I'll deal with you when we get to Glen Cove."

She closed her eyes and leaned back against the velvet head-rest, while Ormley, who was sitting on one of the seats facing us, stared at me. *I* stared at the little crystal vase that hung between the window and the car door.

I reasoned that he must have telephoned my mother to inform her that I was at the Schilling house. He may have seen me at the parlor window, and realized that I had spotted him. When he saw all the lights go off he must have known that I intended to spend the night there—but how could he have known I didn't live there? He needed to enlist my mother's help; she wouldn't hesitate to announce her presence to Oliver, and then nothing would stop her from dragging me off. I learned later that she'd risen early, driven into the city, and arrived just in time to follow my cab.

As the surprise of my capture wore off, rage began to take over, and had there been a weapon handy, even Aunt Eulalia's handbag, I think I would have flung it at Ormley a second time as he sat gloating over his successful entrapment of me. That's how I felt, trapped, and I could see no way to escape. I knew that whatever plans my mother had for me would be difficult, nay, next to impossible, to circumvent.

How right I was! When we arrived at Glen Cove she announced that she would see me in the drawing room at four in the afternoon, and until that time I was to remain in my room. Even though she didn't warn me not to try to leave, I knew from her tone that any such attempt would prove futile. I was not surprised, therefore, when I saw a strange young man seated in the alcove opposite my bedroom door, apparently engrossed in a copy of the *National Geographic* magazine.

After a while my suitcases were brought up (I suppose Mother had gone through them to make sure there were no dangerous weapons in them), but I had no interest in unpacking. I stood at the window looking out at the late-summer flowers in their carefully tended beds, going over the same old question: Why would any sane woman want to force her daughter into an unwanted marriage for the sake of a title? She couldn't be in her right mind if she was willing to condemn me to a lifetime of misery in order to enhance her own social position. Ormley's motive, on the other hand, was obvious: money.

While I waited alone in my room for the summons to the drawing room on that ominously quiet August afternoon, I knew that I would give almost anything to have been free of my mother. I did not consciously wish for her death, but the thought occurred to me that if she *should* die, my life would be far simpler.

The hours passed slowly; lunch was brought up by a maid I had never seen before (that in itself was not unusual, since our summer help changed from year to year), and caused me to wonder what Mollie and Mrs. Groome knew of my situation. I was sure I could count on their sympathy, but I didn't see how they could help me. What about Father? Where was he? Surely not at the bank on a Saturday afternoon. Exhausted by questions to which I could find no answers, I flung myself down under the ruffled canopy of the large tester bed, feeling close to despair. I was too restless to stay there for more than a few minutes, though. Instead I bathed, arranged my hair, and put on one of the afternoon dresses that hung in a neat row in my closet.

At two minutes before four o'clock the same maid knocked

on my door. The young man in the alcove put aside his magazine and followed me as I went slowly down the wide, curving staircase, hoping against hope that my father would be in the drawing room.

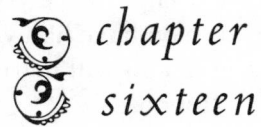
"And she was actually working in that Foundling Hospital until I put a stop to it," I heard Mother say as I opened the door.

There was a silence as I entered the room. "Good afternoon," I said as coldly as I could to the three people who turned to face me. I heard the door close behind me, and knew that without a doubt my guard would be stationed outside it to prevent my leaving. I glanced at the French doors that led to the side terrace, which were usually wide open on a summer day, and was not surprised to see them firmly shut.

"And a very good afternoon to you, Miss Maida," Lord Delcannon said unctuously as he rose from one of the sofas. "As usual, you look lovelier than the rarest of roses."

"I second that," Ormley said, "but—"

"Maida," my mother interrupted quickly, as if to forestall what surely would have been a banal reference to thorns. "Maida, there are several things we must discuss. Come, sit over here, and listen to what I have to say."

I moved slowly across the room and pulled a straight chair into such a position that I faced the three of them, but still kept as much distance as possible between us. Then, without waiting for whatever she had to say (as if I didn't already know), I burst out:

"I will not have anything to do with Viscount Ormley! He threatened to compromise me! Did you know that, Mother?"

"Maida!" my mother snapped. "You will be quiet while I speak, do you understand?" She paused, and stared hard at me for a moment before continuing. "I do not know where you have been, or what you have been doing, but whatever it is, it is over. You have had your rebellion, and it is time to settle your future. You will marry—"

"I won't!"

"Yes, you will! You nearly killed the poor viscount, and you owe it to him, morally and legally—"

"No, no, no! I'll kill myself first! I'll run away! He threatened me!"

I jumped up from the chair, not knowing where I intended to go, just as the door from the hall opened and Father strode into the room. With tears streaming down my face I ran to him, and, like the desperate victim of a shipwreck holding on to a floating log, wound my arms around his neck and clung to him for dear life.

"Don't let them!" I sobbed as he held me, patting my back soothingly. "Don't, don't—"

"No, no, of course not," he said, taking in the situation immediately. "Trust me, my dear. There, there . . ."

"Julian!" My mother's voice was sharp. "Julian! What are you doing here? Why are you not in Europe with Richard Rellenbach? It was arranged—"

"I chose to return, Eleanora," he broke in, "and it seems that I have arrived in the nick of time. Am I correct in assuming that you intend to go ahead with your plan to force Maida to marry against her wishes?"

"Julian! Have you forgotten your manners? Have you no greeting for our guests?"

Father was saved from making what I suspect would have been a discourteous or even insulting reply by what sounded like a commotion in the hall. A moment later Collins opened the door and announced in a disapproving voice that a Mr. Schilling wished to return an earring to a Miss Mary Wick.

What surprised me more than Mr. Schilling's appearance (with the devoted Oliver close behind him) was my father's unexpected reaction to the newcomers.

"Why, Gus Schilling, you old rascal!" he exclaimed, disengaging himself from me. "Am I glad to see you! May I present my wife, Eleanora, and our guests, the Earl of Delcannon and his son, the Viscount Ormley? Gus, Eleanora, is one of my oldest friends. We were at school together, and then at Yale. Sit down, Gus, and tell me, what brings you to Glen Cove?"

"The earring, Julian, the earring. You see, she lost it—must have fallen off—Oliver found it. Miss Wick, it's—you see, it's opals. Oh, Miss Wick! Oliver, where—oh dear."

"Calm down, Gus," Father said gently, "and explain. What is this about an earring, and who is Miss Wick? One of the maids?"

"Oh dear me, no! Not Miss Wick!" And Mr. Schilling looked hopelessly at Oliver, who stepped quickly forward.

"Perhaps I could explain, Mr. Jardine?"

"I wish you would, Oliver," Father said with a sigh. "I have no idea what is going on."

"You see, sir," Oliver began, "we knew your daughter as Miss Wick. She worked on the translations—"

"And very well, too," Mr. Schilling interrupted. "She did a fine job."

"I found the earring," Oliver continued, "just as she left this morning, and by the time I rushed to the front door with it, she was in the cab and didn't hear me call out to her."

"Then I said, 'Follow her, follow her,' " Mr. Schilling said excitedly.

"Yes, sir, you did. And I did. And I was fortunate enough to catch another cab at the corner, and the driver, who said he liked nothing better than a chase, kept her cab in view all the way down Park Avenue, and we were in time to see it draw up in front of a building on Forty-eighth Street. I saw Miss Wick get out of her taxi, and the next thing I knew she was being escorted into a large black limousine. Since I had not completed my mission, I had my driver follow the limousine here."

"Quite right, Oliver, quite right," Mr. Schilling said, nodding his head vigorously.

"But when I appeared at the door I was told that there was no person named Miss Wick in this household. What to do? Mr. Schilling would know! So back to Seventy-fourth Street I went. I am not sure why I told the driver to wait, but it was a good thing that I did, for as soon as I had made my report to Mr. Schilling, he said, 'We'll find her!' and in no time we were in the cab again and on our way here. And here is your earring, Miss Wick. No harm has come to it."

After Oliver had put the earring in my hand I looked around the room, conscious of several pairs of eyes fastened on me, waiting for an explanation. I turned away from the cold gaze of my mother, the puzzled expression of the earl, and the frown of the viscount. Slowly and carefully I directed the account of my employment by Mr. Schilling to my father, who seemed to have trouble suppressing a smile. I did not go into great detail, nor did I give any reason for changing my name to Mary Wick. Nobody asked me for one, either.

Perhaps because of the presence of Mr. Schilling and Oliver (invited by Father to spend the night instead of undertaking yet another long taxi ride), nothing was said about my mother's plans for me that evening. Just before we went to bed, however, Father reminded us that he would see me, Lord Delcannon, Ormley, and my mother in his study the next morning at ten o'clock.

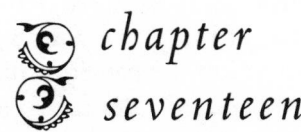 *chapter*
seventeen

The honking of the wild geese flying over the Sound woke me early the next day, and as I lay listening to them call to one another, I replayed in my mind the scene that had taken place in the drawing room the previous afternoon. I wondered what my mother's next move would be. That she would not give up on her plan to marry me to Ormley was a certainty, but would she be able to enlist Father's help in persuading me to change my mind? Could he—

A soft knock on the door interrupted my line of thought, and a moment later I heard Mollie's soft Irish voice:

"Oh, Miss Maida dear, are you all right? Mrs. Groome and me, we were that upset! Not knowing what was goin' on and all. Sure, you look foine. Oh, 'tis good to see you, it is!"

She stood next to my bed, clasping and unclasping her hands as she smiled down at me. "And married, are you? How can yer ma want that poor fish for you when yer already wed?"

"Oh, Mollie, don't worry! No, I'm not married yet, and I'm not going to marry any poor fish. I'll tell you and Mrs. Groome all about it later."

"Sure, and you'd better get off that bed. Breakfast is in ten minutes. Come to the kitchen when you can. I mun run now; I just slipped up here to make sure you was all right—what with that young man at yer door and all. He's gone, anyhow, and good riddance to him! Get dressed now, lovey. Mrs. Groome is just after makin' yer favorite muffins to have with her strawberry preserves. Hurry now."

I did hurry, not as anxious for the muffins as I was to see Father and find out what he had in mind. I didn't think he would let Mother have her way; she had looked as astonished as I felt at the masterful way in which he had taken charge of the situation the previous night. It was as if she, who had been the undisputed ruler for so long, had within the space of a few minutes been deposed and relegated to the position of subject. The suddenness of the change in Father's manner, as well as the force behind it, had caught her totally unprepared. I wondered, though, if even now she wasn't gathering *her* forces in order to regain her former position. She was not one to accept defeat lightly, especially if she saw no reason for it.

I know now what caused the amazing reversal in my parents' positions, but at the time I was at much at sea as Mother was, and could only rejoice that the surprising change in my father had occurred when it did. This was not the man who had told me to comply with my mother's wishes, and then retreated behind his newspaper.

I adjusted the sash on my blue muslin morning dress, wondering briefly (out of old habit) if I'd chosen one that would please Mother. After a last glance in the mirror I left the bedroom and started for the stairs just as Lisette came along the hall carrying Mother's breakfast tray. I smiled at her and admired the perfect single rose in the little silver vase next to the covered toast plate, but she merely nodded and went on.

I shrugged and continued on my way to the breakfast room, smiling again at the memory of the rainy afternoon Lisette had caught me opening the jars on Mother's dressing table. She'd startled me so that I'd upset a bottle of perfume, causing the velvety rose-colored carpet to smell of Fleurs d'Amour for weeks. It finally had to be replaced. I remember Father coming into my room to comfort me that night after I'd been sent supperless to bed. He thought I was crying because I was in disgrace, and when I told him it was because I was hungry he smiled and said he'd see what he could do about that. A little while later Mollie had appeared, carrying a plate of chicken sandwiches underneath a pile of folded laundry.

"Hide the dish under the bed, lovey," she whispered, "so's that Frenchwoman won't see it."

No one liked Lisette much, except Mother, I guess.

Delcannon and Ormley evidently had breakfast sent up to their rooms also, so only Father and I and Mr. Schilling were at the table, where my former employer was lavish in his praise of me and philosophical about his egotistical grandfather. At a little after nine o'clock we saw him and Oliver off in the limousine, and then Father and I walked across the lawn down to the narrow strip of sand and pebbles that constituted our beach.

"You'd never guess that Gus was one of the richest men in New York, would you, Maida?" Father asked as we approached the faded beach chairs that had been set out on the end of the boat dock. "Society would swoon if it knew how many millions that shy little old bachelor has. I wouldn't dare tell your mother; she'd insist on 'bringing him out.'"

"He'd be embarrassed to death at one of her receptions," I said. "Probably he'd just send his regrets, though. How did you happen to know him, Father?"

"Oh, as I said last night, we were at school together, and then later he asked me to handle his investments for him. I told him he needed a broker, but he said no, he wanted a banker, and that I should hire a broker if I needed one, but that I should keep him out of it. It's worked out very well. But Maida, that's not what I want to talk about. Tell me: what on earth did you do to Ormley? How did you knock him out? You're such a slip of a girl."

"It was Aunt Eulalia's handbag."

"What? Handbag? What's that got to do with it?"

"Yes, a present from Aunt Eulalia. You see, the night I left I didn't have a suitcase in my room, and that was the biggest thing I could find. I'd never used it; it was too ugly and heavy. When Ormley threatened me—he came at me, ready to grab me—I was so frightened. Oh, Father, he looked as if he was going to force me to—" I shivered in the warm sunlight, and turned away for a moment. "Anyway, I was so desperate that I hit him with the handbag. It had brass strips all around the edges, and I suppose one of the metal corners caught him in the temple. You see, I was still standing on the bottom step of the back stairs, so I was tall enough to reach his head."

"A most vulnerable spot," Father murmured. "And then what did you do? Where did you go? You weren't with Gus the whole time, were you?"

He listened, almost without interruption, to me as I recounted the events that followed my flight from Fifth Avenue, and when I stopped talking he leaned over and kissed me gently on the forehead.

"My hat is off to you, Maida dear, and I am extremely happy to have you here safe and sound. You are a wonderful, brave girl, and not to be wasted on a charlatan like Ormley."

We sat quietly for a few minutes before he glanced at his watch. "Come," he said, standing up and smiling down at me, "it's time we settled this matter once and for all. But before we see the others, tell me, who is this Mark Delaney who rescued you from the fire?"

"He's an attorney, Father, and he says—said—he loved me. I do like him immensely. Maybe I love him; I'm not sure yet, but I think . . . You see, he doesn't know who I really am. To him I am Mary Wick."

"If he loves you, my dear," Father said, putting his arm around my shoulders, "he will love you whoever you are. But come along now, it's almost ten o'clock."

"Julian, what happened to the guard I hired for Maida? The maids say he's gone. Who ordered him to leave?" Mother demanded as she sailed into the study.

The earl looked up from the book he'd taken down from the shelves, and the viscount returned to the desk the paperweight he'd been examining through a small magnifying glass. Both men remained silent and expressionless.

"Sit down, Eleanora," Father said, ignoring her question. "You've kept us waiting a good quarter of an hour, and I, for one, have other business to attend to."

"But Julian—" she began.

"Enough!" Father sounded so emphatic that although she opened her mouth to protest she thought better of it, and pretended to brush a speck of lint from the chair before she seated herself.

The earl sat opposite her, while Ormley ambled over to the sofa against the far wall. Father sat in the upholstered swivel chair behind his desk, and as I pulled the stepstool I'd been perching on closer to him he turned so that the others could see only his profile and winked broadly at me, reminding me for a moment of Jerome. He looks ready to open a board meeting, I thought, and I was wondering how many times he had done just that when the earl cleared his throat nervously.

"Mr. Jardine," he said in the tone one would use to pacify an unreasonable child, "I know that you consider a dowry of two million—"

"I am not here to discuss the amount of any dowry, sir," Father snapped. "Since there will be no marriage, there will be no need of any such discussion. Is that clear?"

"But, my dear sir," the earl persisted. "Think what an opportunity you are passing up! Your daughter would be a countess! Mrs. Jardine understands what a great privilege—"

"A privilege!" Father snorted. "To what manner of privilege are you referring? The privilege of living on a tumbledown estate? One that has gone to rack and ruin?"

He paused and stared hard at the earl.

"Ah, yes, I know all about your ancestral acres; I made a point of visiting them when I was in England last month. Had Mrs. Jardine bothered to check on your bona fides—"

"Julian, what are you saying? He is an earl, isn't he?" Mother sounded distraught.

"I am saying, Eleanora, that earl or no earl, he has misrepresented his social and financial position, as well as his entire manner of living. I am also saying that his son's proposal of marriage to Maida is here and now rejected! Under no circumstances will I permit such a match. That is all I have to say to you, gentlemen, except to urge you to depart at your earliest convenience."

"Just a minute, sir." Ormley spoke for the first time. "What about this?" he asked, tapping the angry scar with a long forefinger. "It surely deserves some recompense."

"Not—one—penny!" Father stood up as he all but spat the words at the viscount. "Let that scar be your payment for your vile behavior."

"Mr. Jardine," the earl said in a carefully controlled voice, "surely you realize that your daughter has disfigured my son beyond repair and is responsible for ruining his chances of making any kind of match, ruined his life, in fact. Can you not see that she is morally obligated to bring him what solace and comfort she can by marrying him?"

"No, I cannot!" Father thundered. "But I can have you forcibly removed if you do not leave my home at once."

"Very well, sir. If that is the position you propose to take, we shall leave at once. I assume transportation will be arranged?" The earl looked at Mother, who inclined her head slightly, but said nothing. He then turned to Father again.

"You will hear from me in due course, sir," he said quietly before following his son out of the room.

"Perhaps you ought to hire a guard to watch them, Eleanora," Father said with a bitter laugh as the door closed behind them. "They may take your diamonds, or Maida's opal earring." He turned and smiled at me.

"Julian," Mother said in a voice that sounded half strangled, "did you really see their estates? Were they truly in ruins?"

"Truly, Eleanora, really and truly, and it would take all of two million to restore them—that is, if that's what they used the money for. I also unearthed the fact that the two of them are inveterate gamblers, and heavily in debt. I'll tell you more about it later. First things first: Michael couldn't be back yet from taking Gus to the city, so will you ring for Collins and have him send for a taxi?"

"Are they really going for good?" I asked, glancing at the door of the study. "I can't believe it! And I can't believe that I don't have to hide any longer—"

"No, you don't, child," Father said gently. "It's all over. Now run along and amuse yourself and think about what you'd like to do from now on. Close the door as you go out; I want to talk to your mother."

Suddenly I felt like a girl again, and after pausing for a moment at the mirror in the hall I hurried down to the kitchen to see Mollie and Mrs. Groome. After a plate of cookies and a cup of coffee (and a lot of excited talk about the "nobles"), I wandered off to the rose garden to think about the future. Father would, I was sure, let me do anything within reason—and, I realized with a start, Mother would no longer have the final word. Whatever had happened to cause the reversal of their positions I still didn't know, and I'm not sure that I was ever meant to know.

By the time the gong sounded for lunch I had decided what I'd like to do. I knew I had been independent of my mother for too long to contemplate living under the same roof with her again; we'd both be miserable. But did I want to live alone? I wasn't sure. I watched a blue jay fly from a branch down to a bird feeder, and for the second time that day I thought of Jerome. Years ago he'd given me a special feeder to hang outside my window for hummingbirds. Jerome was the answer.

"Could I go to Italy and live with Jerome and Maria for a while, Father?" I asked when the maid left the dining room after serving the fish chowder. "You said to think about what I'd like to do."

"Jerome has recently returned to New York," Mother said. "He and his wife and child are in residence on Washington Square, but I have not seen them. He wrote, asking if they could come down here last weekend, but I did not find it convenient."

Father and I looked at each other without speaking. He merely nodded, and began to talk about building a pavilion next to the boathouse.

"Just don't let her find another peer for me," I whispered to him as we followed Mother out of the dining room.

"Not a chance," he replied softly. "I'll talk to Jerome." And he moved ahead of me to catch up with Mother.

Three days later I received a warm letter from Jerome, with an equally warm postscript from Maria, inviting me to move in with them in Washington Square. "It's time you saw something of your niece, little sister," he wrote. "She remembers you clearly (she won't go to bed without the 'Maida doll'). And you'll be company for Maria, who is staying pretty close to home these days."

Fond as I was of Jerome, I wasn't at all sure that I wanted to be wholly dependent on him, to be the relative who must be taken care of, the maiden aunt who is passed around from one branch of the family to another. Father urged me to give it a chance, stressing that the situation need not be considered a permanent one.

"Look at it this way, Maida. Of course you won't live with Jerome forever, just for the time being, while you decide whether you love Mark Delaney or not. And don't worry about being a burden to anyone, my dear. You couldn't be that if you tried. To my mind, however, the most important thing is that you'll be free of your mother's domination."

"Have you mentioned this plan to her? What did she say?"

He chuckled and put his arm around my shoulders as we sauntered down to the water's edge.

"She is so embarrassed, ashamed, really, that she misjudged Delcannon and Ormley so badly that she'll be glad not to have to face you for a while. She looked surprised when I told her about Jerome's proposal, and then she nodded and said she thought such a visit would do you good. Maybe that's the way to look at it, Maida, as a visit."

"I suppose it's the best thing," I said slowly. "It will give us time to try to get over our differences. But Father, I doubt that I will ever forget what she tried to do to me. She's never loved me, not the way you do."

He was silent for a few moments, and then he sighed.

"She's had problems, Maida, things you've never dreamed of. Please, my dear, in spite of what has happened, don't judge her too harshly. She was carried away by an uncontrollable, overriding ambition, and couldn't help herself."

And I was to be sacrificed to that ambition, I thought bitterly, wondering if I could ever forgive her. I had better move out at once, I decided, before I said something hurtful and unnecessary.

"I'll write to Jerome this afternoon," I said, and watched Father nod approvingly. "When do you think I should go?"

"You mean that you never knew that Dr. Risley called on you, Maida?" Sister Mary Veronica looked puzzled as she pushed a plate of little biscuits across her desk toward me. "He said he'd asked you for permission to call, but when he did, and he went twice, he was told you were not at home. I don't remember exactly when it was, but it was after you stopped coming to us, and before you left on the orphan train."

"I'm very sorry about that," I said. "I would have liked to have seen him. Collins, our butler, must have had orders from my mother. She had her eye on the viscount for me then, and wouldn't have wanted anything or anybody to interfere with that. So typical of her . . . Where did you say Dr. Risley went?"

"To Boston. He was offered a splendid position there in the Children's Hospital, Chief of Medicine, a real feather in his cap."

"Perhaps it's just as well that he never reached me, Sister. It wouldn't have done his career any good to have his name associated with that of a suspected criminal," I said, at the same time wondering what Mark Delaney would think if he knew that Mary Wick was really Maida Jardine. I couldn't bring myself to write to him again, afraid of having him turn away from me in disgust.

I *had* started to write to him several times during the six weeks I'd been living in Jerome's house, but the letters were never finished. I had too much to tell and too much explaining to do, and felt unequal to the task. Wouldn't it be better, I wondered, to send him a simple note, asking him to call on me at Washington Square? Then I could watch his reaction as I made clear the reasons for my assumed name and my sudden disappearance.

Jerome and Maria had been deeply impressed when I told them how Mark had rescued me from the Triangle fire, and I was sure they'd be happy to welcome him.

I'll tell them tonight that I'd like to invite him, I thought as I rode downtown on the elevated train, after I've gotten Christina off to bed.

She'd be waiting for me, I knew, to come home from the Foundling Hospital—where once more I was spending several afternoons a week—waiting for me to tell her yet another story about an adventurous kitten named Mike while she ate her supper. She was a dear child, and I loved the time I spent with her when Maria was resting (she was in the early stages of pregnancy) or when the nurse had her day off.

I remember tucking Christina into bed that night and being called back twice to make sure the Maida doll was properly covered before I could slip out of the room with a final good night. I changed quickly into a new maroon silk dress (Father had given me a more than generous allowance), and hurried down the stairs just as the maid was answering the front-door bell.

"Father! How good to see you!" I exclaimed, putting my face up for his kiss. "I didn't know you were coming for dinner tonight."

"I didn't either, my dear, until noontime today. Jerome thought I'd better come and tell you myself."

"Tell me what? What on earth—"

"Nothing we can't handle," he said quickly, and taking my arm he led me into the parlor, where Jerome and Maria were waiting.

"No, nothing we can't handle," Father repeated after greeting my brother and his wife. "Nothing to worry about."

"What is it?" I asked impatiently. "Is Mother—"

"No, no—well, here it is: those despicable Delcannons have gone to law. They have brought suit against us. I'll get the best lawyers I can. I've already asked John Prendergast to recommend a firm that specializes in this kind of case, and—"

"The whole thing is preposterous," Jerome murmured. "Suing for breach of promise when Maida never agreed to marry the fellow in the first place."

"They are not only suing for breach of promise, Jerome," Father said, "but also for permanent disfigurement of the viscount by means of unreasonable force. In other words, for assault and battery."

"How could it be called unreasonable force when a young girl merely used a handbag to ward off her attacker?" Maria asked. "When I was working at Saint Luke's Hospital I saw a nurse stab an orderly with a pair of surgical scissors when he made unwelcome advances to her. He was dismissed, and nothing at all happened to her."

"As you say, Maria, you saw it happen. She had at least one witness," Father said, "and therefore the orderly didn't dare sue. Or maybe he felt he was in no position to do so. In our case there were no witnesses, and Ormley has the scar to show as evidence. As I see it, it will be up to our lawyers to prove that what Maida did was entirely in self-defense, and that the handbag was not a weapon, a gun or a knife, for instance, or even a pair of scissors. Jerome, pour me a large Scotch, will you?"

"Of course, Father," Jerome said, moving toward the liquor cabinet. "A sherry for you, Maida?" I nodded, and we were quiet while he handed the drinks around.

"Couldn't it be settled out of court?" Maria asked after a moment or two.

"I might have considered settling one way or another, Maria, if they hadn't already published their intention to sue. Have you seen the evening paper? There's one in my coat pocket out in the hall."

The headline on the front page left no doubt in our minds about the intentions of Delcannon and Ormley:

WOUNDED VISCOUNT SUES JARDINES
SUIT FOR ASSAULT AND BREACH OF PROMISE STUNS CITY
HEIRESS AT FAULT

Viscount Ormley, son and heir of the Earl of Delcannon, hovered between life and death for several weeks after being attacked by Miss Maida Jardine, youngest daughter of financier Julian Jardine. Until the viscount regained consciousness and remembered being struck by Miss Jardine, it was assumed that his assailant had been an intruder into the Jardine home on Fifth Avenue. Miss Jardine, who was rumored to be engaged to be married to the viscount, disappeared on the night in question, February 15 of this year, and has only recently returned to the city. No date has as yet been set for the trial.

"The press neglected to state that the suit is for two million dollars," Father said after we had all read the column, "and that, to my mind, leaves us no choice but to contest. If we do not, we are admitting, at least in the eyes of the public, that we are at fault, which we are not. No, I cannot countenance any settlement that would result in a stigma on Maida or any member of my family."

He must have been thinking of Mother when he said that. It was she, after all, who had dealt with and encouraged Delcannon and Ormley, and who had urged me to accept the proposal.

"However it turns out," Father continued after a moment's pause, "it will not be a pleasant experience for any of us. God knows what accusations Delcannon and Ormley will make, or to what scurrility they will stoop. The fact that you left the city, Maida—which was entirely my doing—will not help our case. They will construe that as evidence of guilt, and we must be able to counteract it."

Dinner was announced at that point, and although we all tried to talk about things unrelated to the news in the paper, it was a quiet meal. Father and Jerome didn't linger over their port that night, but followed Maria and me into the parlor for coffee immediately after dessert. We were quiet there, too, and Father didn't stay long.

"You are not to worry, my dear," he said to me as he prepared to leave. "You'll see; this will come out all right in the end."

I wanted to believe him, but his tone didn't sound convincing to me, and as I went up to bed that night I felt that the cloud that had been so wonderfully dispersed in Glen Cove six weeks ago with the departure of the earl and his son had suddenly returned here in New York, larger and darker than ever.

Father's prediction that Delcannon and his son would stop at nothing was borne out; they, or rather their lawyers, lost no opportunity to twist and turn my slightest action so that it appeared to be malicious or, in the worst case, criminal. However, Mr. Simms, of the firm of Simms and Forsyte, had tried to prepare me for the questioning I would have to undergo in court. I was closeted with him for hours on end, going over the list of witnesses the lawyers for the plaintiff intended to call, trying to anticipate what might be derogatory in their testimony.

At first I couldn't imagine how they had found out so much about me, how they had located not only Mr. Brookfield, of the orphan train, but also Arnold Iverson of Redfield, Michigan, but then I remembered overhearing Mother's remark to the earl as I entered the drawing room in Glen Cove: "And she was working in that Foundling place."

Mr. Simms nodded when I told him that. "Of course, that's how it was done," he said. "They put a detective to work, and he traced you from the Foundling to the Children's Aid Society. Now, Miss Jardine, as I understand it, when you returned from Redfield, your next step was to work for the Triangle Shirtwaist Factory, and after the fire there you found employment with Mr. Augustus Schilling. We know he will vouch for your character, but can you think of anyone else who would stand up for you? And who is this Reggie Gardner they've got on their list? Friend or foe?"

"Friend, I would think," I answered after taking a moment to place the young man I'd seen at various affairs after I came out. "I've danced with him at parties, but I can't say I know him well. He never talked about anything but his polo ponies."

"Well, we'll have to wait and see. Now, what about someone at Triangle?"

"I wasn't there very long, and the only one I can think of is Josephine Nicolini, a girl who worked near me. I went to her house twice, and her family seemed to like me. Oh, Mr. Simms, Sister Mary Veronica and Sister Agnes at the Foundling would vouch for me. Are nuns allowed to come to court?"

"I'll find out. It depends on the rules of the order. If they are not permitted to appear, or cannot be absent from their responsibilities, we'll have depositions taken, and they can be presented in court."

At the thought of the two good sisters coming to my rescue I suddenly smiled, and felt more confident than I had of late. Mr. Simms noticed the change in my expression, and leaned over to pat my hand.

"Good!" he said. "I am happy to see you perking up. It's important that you present a calm exterior to the jury, even if the opposition tried to rattle you. Any appearance of worry or uncertainty could be interpreted as stemming from a guilty conscience, which, of course, wouldn't be the case here. I think we're about ready, Miss Jardine, to win this case."

The highly publicized trial, which did not begin until the first week of November, lasted for fifteen days, fifteen long, long days. I cannot possibly remember everything that was said during that fortnight, but certain things, the things that struck me as important, I shall never forget.

Viscount Ormley took the stand early in the proceedings. He claimed that I had not only broken my promise to marry him, but had also grievously injured him. Here he pointed to the scar on his forehead. When Mr. Simms asked him how he happened to be in the kitchen of our house on the night of February 15, or rather, on the morning of the sixteenth, he replied that he had called at the Jardine house on the evening of the fifteenth, and that he and Mrs. Jardine had talked at length.

"The hour was late, nearly midnight," he said, "and the weather so inclement that Mrs. Jardine invited me to spend the night in one of the guest rooms on the third floor. I accepted gratefully, but after I had been upstairs for a while I realized I was not at all sleepy, and went down to the kitchen hoping I could find the makings of a toddy to help send me off."

"And when Miss Jardine came down the back stairs she found you in a rocking chair?"

"That's nonsense!" Ormley exclaimed. "I was on my feet, looking for the whiskey."

"What did you say to Miss Jardine?"

"I said nothing, sir. Before I could speak, she hit me with that handbag, the one over there on the table, and I remember nothing after that."

There was a pause then, while Aunt Eulalia's handbag was passed around to the members of the jury so that they could examine it. Then Ormley was asked to step down, and I was called upon to give my version of what happened. I explained that he *had* been sitting in the rocking chair, waiting until he was sure I was asleep, and how he had come at me, threatening to compromise me so that I would have to marry him, and how I had swung the handbag at him so that I could get away from him. There was a moment's silence in the court, and I could almost hear the members of the jury saying to themselves: Well, it's her word against his. Which one is to be believed?

Then Ormley's lawyers went into action, determined to represent me as a wanton. I couldn't believe my ears when I heard Arnold Iverson testify that on two occasions I had tried to lure him into my bed during the blizzard in Redfield! And Mrs. Iverson was no help to me at all; when Mr. Simms questioned her, all she would say was that she'd heard her husband get up in the night, but that she assumed he was going downstairs for a glass of warm milk, something he often did. She probably was afraid to tell the truth; she knew how brutal he could be.

When it was my turn to be questioned on the matter, I stated that I thought someone had tried to open my door one night during the storm, but that I had no idea who it was until the next day, when I overheard Mrs. Iverson accuse her husband of approaching me.

"And what did Mr. Iverson say to that accusation?" Mr. Simms asked.

"I didn't hear him *say* anything," I answered, "but I did hear what sounded like a slap—no, a blow—and then Mrs. Iverson cried out."

At that point Arnold Iverson shouted that I was a liar, and shook his fist at me. Several of the spectators became noisy, and the judge threatened to clear the court if quiet was not restored. I had no idea which one of us the jury believed; I didn't dare look at them, but was sitting with my eyes lowered, waiting to see what would happen next, when court was abruptly adjourned until the following morning.

*   *   *

My mother, of course, had not been in court at all, and that night at dinner I asked Father how she was taking it all.

"She's not here, Maida," he answered. "As soon as she saw those first headlines, the ones I showed you, she went on a cruise to Rio de Janeiro and God knows where else with a party that Rellenbach organized."

"But Father, she's the one who made Ormley think I'd marry him! Won't the lawyers want to question her? Won't Mr. Simms—"

"Simms did speak to me about her. He wanted her to testify, but since she's out of the country . . . oh, even if she weren't, she wouldn't appear. She'd get some doctor to swear that she was too ill."

"Excuse me, Miss Maida." The young parlormaid stood in the doorway looking perplexed. "There's a Mr. Delaney here who says he must see you. I asked him to wait in the parlor."

I excused myself, and after a glance at the amused expression on Father's face walked as slowly as I could out of the dining room and down the hall to the parlor. Mark was warming his hands at the glowing coals in the fireplace. I stood still in the doorway until he turned, and when his eyes lighted up as he came toward me, a wave of relief, strong enough to cause tears to spring to my eyes, swept over me.

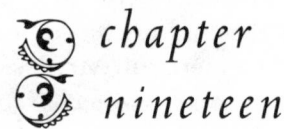# chapter
nineteen

"Mark! Oh Mark! I was going to write you a note," I said when I could speak, "but I was afraid—"

"Afraid of what, my darling? You know that I love you. Nothing can change that. But I was puzzled—and worried—when you simply disappeared. And then I didn't hear from you—why didn't you come to me? Tell me—"

"There was . . . is . . . so much you don't know about me, things I've been afraid to mention. I'll tell you now, but first you tell me how you managed to find me."

"Your picture in the newspaper, darling," he said with a laugh. "The moment I saw it I knew that Maida Jardine was the Mary Wick I had known. I went to the Jardine house on Fifth Avenue at once, and the maid told me you were living here."

It's a good thing, I thought, that the parlormaid had opened the door for him; Collins would never have given him Jerome's address. "And you came directly here?" I asked.

"As fast as I could," he replied. "Now, tell me where you've been, and fill me in on the details of this preposterous case. Perhaps I can help."

Although Mark's arrival did wonders for my *amour propre*—just knowing that he still loved me did that—I worried constantly about the outcome of the trial. In a civil suit like this one, Mr. Simms said, the penalty could be only a financial one if the verdict went against us; there was no possibility of my being sentenced to a prison term. But what if Father couldn't raise two million dollars without leaving himself penniless? Would Mother help? I rather thought not . . .

As the trial proceeded I began to feel hopeful that the jury would be merciful. Mr. Jackson, the attorney for the plaintiff, called only one more character witness after Mrs. Iverson was excused. Reggie Gardner (who I had thought would be on my side) remembered that he had seen me dining with Mark one night last summer, and said that the two of us seemed to be engaged in intimate conversation, and that I gave every appearance of being a flirtatious woman. Apparently he was annoyed that I had refused to recognize him that night. Once more I kept my eyes lowered and refrained from glancing at the jury.

I watched carefully, though, as Mr. Simms called the witnesses in my defense. Mr. Brookfield, or Mr. B., as the orphans and I had called him, was full of praise for the way I had handled the children on the trip to Redfield, Michigan, and said he believed implicitly my version of what happened in the Iverson home. Then Josie Nicolini was called. She remained calm under Mr. Simms's gentle questioning, but under cross-examination she became so emotional that I was afraid the judge would find her out of order. Sister Mary Veronica and Sister Agnes were unable to appear in court, but the depositions Mr. Simms had taken, both of them decidedly supportive of me, were read and admitted as evidence.

And dear Mr. Schilling! He had nothing but the best to say of me, but in his desire to give detailed examples of the excellence of the work I had done for him, he took forever to answer a question. Twice Mr. Simms found it necessary to stop him from recounting the entire plot of *The Old Castle* and the subsequent search for the ruby. Ormley's attorney didn't bother to cross-examine him. Mr. Jackson was, I realize now, holding his fire.

The next day he put Ormley on the stand again, and requested him to brush back his hair so that the jury could see the "angry scar" (his words) in its entirety. Then he picked up Aunt Eulalia's handbag and proceeded to demonstrate to the jury just how it could be used as a dangerous weapon. Mr. Simms objected, but he was overruled.

Then Mr. Jackson questioned me at length. I was exhausted, almost numb by the end of that day. I had to explain over and over again that I was running away to avoid an undesirable marriage, why I changed my name first to Mary Wicklow and then to Mary Wick, and why, when I surprised Ormley in the kitchen, I swung my handbag at him.

"I am sorry that he was badly hurt," I said. "I had no desire to injure him; I just wanted him to stay away from me."

At that there was a subdued murmur in the courtroom, but I had no idea how to interpret it.

"Mr. Simms," the judge said wearily, "we will begin with you tomorrow."

"There's something strange about that scar," Mark said as he sat with us in the parlor that night.

"How do you mean?" Jerome asked.

"It's the size of it. Haven't you noticed? Or maybe it's the shape," Mark answered. "Until I saw the handbag I thought—I mean I really hadn't given it any thought at all until then. However, it seems to me now that the metal corner of that bag couldn't possibly have made a cut more than an inch long, if that. And yet his scar extends halfway across his forehead."

"That's it! Mark, you've got it!" Jerome cried excitedly, jumping up from his chair to shake Mark's hand. "The fellow cut himself deliberately, or had it done. It's like the dueling scar, the German Schmiss, a mark of honor! He wanted to exaggerate his injury."

"Father, could it be . . ." I began.

"Yes, my dear, I think it could. We ought to inform Simms of this at once, tell him to arrange for a physician's opinion, to have a physician in court. Mark, I saw you talking to Simms today; can you reach him tonight, do you think?"

As we expected, Ormley and his lawyers objected to an examination of the scar by a doctor, but in the end they were obliged to permit one by a court-appointed physician. There was not a sound in the courtroom when the viscount and his attorney returned from the judge's chambers, where the examination had taken place, and we sat in silence while we waited for the physician to appear with his report.

When at last Dr. Mackenzie, a short, gray-haired Scotsman, walked slowly up to the witness stand, the atmosphere of suspense that had been building up in the courtroom was almost palpable. I was wondering how much longer I could stand it when he adjusted his spectacles and began to read from a small notebook.

"I have examined the weapon, the handbag, that is," he read slowly, "and I have examined the scar on the plaintiff's forehead. I must ask the court to allow me to defer my final report until after I have made inquiries at Bellevue Hospital, and conferred with the surgeon who attended Mr.—excuse me—Viscount Ormley."

"How much time do you need, Dr. Mackenzie?" the judge asked.

"I can't say for sure," the doctor replied, "but if all goes well, if I can get at the records this evening, I should be able to summarize in the morning."

"This court will reconvene at ten o'clock tomorrow," the judge announced, and as he left the bench I felt like joining in the buzz of disappointment that filled the room. Somehow or other I will have to get through a long night, I thought, turning to watch Mr. Simms gather up his papers.

"Cheer up, my dear," he said after glancing at my face. "It looks promising, thanks to young Delaney—oh, here he is now. What do you think, sir?"

"I feel sure the jury will find for Maida, Mr. Simms," Mark said with a smile. "I feel like celebrating at once."

"I do, too," Mr. Simms said, "but it might, just might, be a bit premature. Best to wait. Now, off with you. Put it all out of your minds for tonight, and be here on time in the morning."

Strangely enough, I was almost able to forget about the trial that night, perhaps because I kept remembering how Mark had kissed me when he said good night, and how wonderful it felt to be held in his arms, if only for a few moments.

"My considered opinion," Dr. Mackenzie said as soon as the court reconvened the next day, "and Dr. Springer of Bellevue Hospital concurs, is that Viscount Ormley suffered not one but two separate wounds, so close together that they might be mistaken for a single one. The one made by the handbag in question is obviously a stellate laceration, with five points radiating from a common center. Adjacent to it is a linear laceration, which could only have been made by a scalpel, a knife, or some other sharp blade. It could not possibly have been made by the instrument that caused the stellate laceration.

"Unfortunately, the physician who attended the viscount in February died in a boating accident off Nantucket last summer, so we do not have his testimony. We do, however, have his notes, from which it is obvious that he treated one wound as stellate and the other as linear. I consulted two other physicians at Bellevue as well as Dr. Springer, and we are all four in agreement in this matter."

After that, things happened fairly quickly: Ormley, in desperation, claimed that I had caused both wounds—after all, he said, there were plenty of sharp knives in the kitchen, and he insisted that I had broken my promise to marry him, all of which I denied calmly and firmly. Then his attorney, Mr. Jackson, summed up the case for the plaintiff, and Mr. Simms for the defense, and the judge instructed the jury in their duty. All during their deliberation, which took the better part of the afternoon, I could only think that it was still my word against Ormley's, and hope that I'd be the one they'd believe.

It was almost five o'clock when the jury returned to a courtroom that was once more almost eerily silent. The note the foreman handed the bailiff stated that the jury found me innocent of any breach of promise, and not guilty of intentional assault. They found me liable only for the medical expenses incurred in the treatment of the stellate laceration, but these damages were not to exceed the sum of five hundred dollars.

To my surprise the spectators applauded, and then Father hugged me, Jerome hugged me, even Mr. Simms hugged me, and Mark swept me up in his arms and kissed me.

"We'll celebrate," he exclaimed, keeping me close to him. "Where would you like to go, my darling?"

"I've set it all up, Mark," Jerome said. "The party is at my house, ready to start."

And what a party it was! Mr. Schilling came, bringing Oliver with him; Josie came with her husband Roberto; Mr. Simms brought his wife; Mr. Brookfield came alone; and little Christina was allowed to stay up long enough to meet them all. Jerome and Maria were the perfect host and hostess, and Father went out of his way to see that everyone was having a good time. My brother Henry and my sister Alicia, who had been conspicuously absent from the courtroom, telephoned congratulations, but no one felt like talking very long to either of them.

After most of the guests had gone, I returned from seeing Mr. Schilling and Oliver off to find Mark waiting for me in the parlor.

"Maria was tired, so Jerome took her upstairs," he said,

"and you must be tired, too, Maida—Maida! You know, that name suits you."

"Shall we sit down, Mark? Would you like . . ." I was on the point of offering him a nightcap when he interrupted me.

"What I'd like is—Maida, I love you! I want to marry you! Do you . . . will you . . ."

I barely had time to smile and nod my head before he enveloped me in his arms and kissed me passionately on the lips, and then tenderly on my face and neck.

"I knew from the beginning, darling, that I couldn't live without you," he said after a while. We were sitting on the sofa, his right arm holding me close to him while his left hand held both of mine. "I thought I'd go crazy when I didn't hear from you."

"I kept trying to write, Mark, but I was afraid you wouldn't understand why I posed as Mary Wick—"

"Darling, Mary Wick or Maida Jardine—it doesn't matter. I love *you!*"

Just what Father had said, I thought, putting my face up to be kissed. "I love you, Mark Delaney, and I'll marry you as soon—"

He didn't let me finish, and I didn't care.

Today, January 12, 1962, is our fiftieth anniversary, and not surprisingly my mind keeps going back not only to that bright sunny day in 1912 when Mark and I were married, but also to the years that followed and the startling discovery I made after my father's death in 1922.

After a honeymoon trip to Mexico on the SS *Morro Castle* and a visit with Mark's parents in the nation's capital, we stayed in a suite in the Fifth Avenue Hotel while I set about furnishing the four-story house on Eighty-second Street that Father gave us for a wedding present.

"It may seem too large for you and Mark just now," he said with a chuckle on one of his regular Sunday-afternoon visits. "But wait! The time will come when you'll fill it up and might even need more room."

He was right; we did indeed fill it up, and rather rapidly. By 1917 we had three boys, Jules, Richard, and Lawrence, and in 1919, exactly nine months after Mark returned from the fighting in France, Veronica was born.

Over the years Jerome has been the only one of my siblings with whom we've had a warm relationship. Henry and Grace

have been cordial, especially since Mark was made a full partner in his firm, but my sister Alicia and her husband Stanley are
far too busy seeking remedies for their aches and pains at one
spa after another to be interested in us. Lenore, of course, is in
Europe, and rarely comes to visit, while Peter seems content to
stay in the Carolinas.

Father continued to live in the Fifth Avenue house after
Mother's death in the fall of 1912. She'd had some sort of nervous breakdown while on the cruise with the Rellenbach party
the previous winter (probably a stroke, Henry said), and had
been an invalid for several months before she died. I went to see
her early in her illness, but she only stared at me blankly for a
moment before turning her face away. I did not repeat the visit,
but I went to her funeral to please Father.

I thought he would be more comfortable in a smaller establishment than the large, now empty, Fifth Avenue house, but
when I suggested it he shook his head.

"It's too much trouble to move, my dear," he said, "and as
for convenience, I have everything I need right here. It's an
ideal place for entertaining my friends, and I am able to put up
out-of-town guests without having to worry if there are enough
sheets and blankets; your mother saw to all that. I have, however, closed off her rooms for the time being. Too many memories there."

I had noticed the locked doors one afternoon when I went
back to clear out my old bedroom of personal possessions.
Some of the same scents I had known as a child still lingered
faintly on the second floor, tenuous reminders of the extrava-
gances of the past. Mark and I live far more conservatively.

When Father died in 1922 at the age of seventy-five, we found
that he had stipulated in his will that his house was to be sold,
but not until I had had ample time to go through it and take for
myself whatever objects I wanted. I also inherited the Glen
Cove house, where we now live year-round. Mark says that if

we are ever in dire need of funds we can rent out the ten guest rooms to weekenders or summer vacationers. The rest of Father's estate, aside from a few small bequests, was divided evenly among his six children, share and share alike, and fortunately there were no arguments or complaints from anyone.

Shortly after his death I spent an afternoon going through the books in his study to see which ones I would like to have for myself. There wasn't anything else in the house I wanted to take, to the dismay of Mollie and Mrs. Groome, who thought I ought to have the silver, the best china, and God knows what else. Alicia took most of that, although where she put it I can't imagine.

After stacking the books that I wanted in a corner of the study, I sat down to rest at the desk where I'd so often seen Father writing in his journal. I opened one of the drawers and was idly thumbing through a pile of folders relating to household accounts when I came across a large envelope containing a long letter addressed to me, which I include in this memoir.

Since these pages are undated, I have no way of knowing when they were written, but judging from the contents I am inclined to think that very little time elapsed after the events he describes before he took up his pen. Nor do I know why he kept them hidden away. Did he intend to destroy the letter at some time? In any case, I am including it here for two reasons: first, although I was shocked beyond measure by what I read, it enabled me to understand why my young life took the path it did; and second, because what Father wrote reveals his character in a way that could not be accomplished by another, no matter how keen his powers of observation or how facile his pen.

Was it his intention that I find the letter? Is that why he stipulated that the house should not be sold until I had taken what I wanted? Was this his way of telling me what he thought I should know? Or had he forgotten that the pages were in the bottom drawer of his desk?

Maida, my dearest child,

The following pages may help you understand why certain events in the past took the course they did. You may despise me when you finish reading them, but that is a risk I shall have to take, unless I decide to destroy them.

When Richard Rellenbach asked me to accompany him to Europe on the *Sequoia* in August 1911, I felt that I had been commanded rather than invited to make the trip with him. Although I had been careful during the long years of our business association not ever to put myself under obligation to the old man, I was incapable, as were so many others, of ignoring the knowledge that within his grasp lay the power to ruin anyone to whom he took even a slight dislike.

I'd seen it happen at least three times: Simon Brand lost his shirt after an argument at a directors' meeting. No one is sure just what Rellenbach did, but a week later Brand's company declared bankruptcy. Bob Truscott was forced out of the presidency of the Moreland Bank, and here the story was that he had refused to approve a merger proposed by Rellenbach. And poor Scott Allgood left town after an altercation with Rellenbach concerning his share of the profits in an operation he had worked on. There were other stories, too . . .

When exactly the old man (he must have been at least seventy then) came to be such a close friend of my wife's, I do not know, but now that I think of it, they did spend a good deal of time together when we went on that Caribbean cruise several years ago. Eleanora reveled in the luxury the yacht afforded, and made sure her acquaintances heard long descriptions of the appointments, the service, and the beauty of what was said to be the largest privately owned yacht in the country at that time.

But what on earth attracted him to her? Granted that Eleanora was an exceptionally handsome woman, at least before she became ill, she didn't know a stock from a bond, and had no head whatsoever for business, which is all that Rellenbach was interested in, that and poker. And yet I saw him bending gallantly toward her over the teacups, listening intently to what she had to say.

Oh, he is by no means the only one to have become enslaved by her beauty; men always danced attendance on her, and I remember only too well how completely I fell under her spell in the spring of 1873. The strange thing was that I didn't really like her very much, even then. But could I keep away from her? No, I could not. I didn't even try, although my common sense told me to flee. Circe comes to mind . . .

I have no doubt that it was she who put Rellenbach up to "inviting" me on that trip; she wanted no interference from me in any plans she was making to find you. She wanted me out of the way so that she and Ormley could pursue their search unimpeded, hiring detectives and all. And of course she may have suspected that I played some part in our daughter's disappearance. I've been extremely circumspect, but Eleanora was not stupid.

In any event, I went on the trip with Rellenbach. I cannot say I enjoyed it; I simply endured it. It was comfortable enough, more than comfortable on that huge, luxurious ship, but the heavy food (which was difficult to avoid without offending our host), the long nightly games of poker, accompanied by large quantities of whiskey and brandy, exhausted me. I cannot speak for the other four guests, but I for one took no pleasure in what conversation there was on those occasions, consisting as it did of banalities and ribaldry.

During the daytime hours, however, there were no planned activities aboard ship. We were expected to appear promptly at meals, but aside from that were left to amuse or entertain ourselves as we saw fit.

I cannot begin to estimate the amount of money that was poured into the furnishing of that magnificent two-hundred-and-sixty-foot steam yacht. The main saloon—the drawing room, in fact, with its carved stone fireplace, silken wall covering, and Louis Quinze furniture—alone must have cost the better part of a million. Then there were the delicate, valuable ornaments, Dresden shepherdesses and the like, which stood about on every available surface. I was told they had their own specially made wooden boxes in which they were carefully packed away at the first sign of rough weather. They were, I suspect, worth another fortune.

The dining saloon, with its massive mahogany furniture, could easily have accommodated twenty guests, but had been rearranged so that the six of us were not lost in it. Needless to say, the gold-rimmed monogrammed china was of the highest quality, Limoges, I believe. The staterooms, too, were elegantly appointed; mine boasted a canopied bed, a writing desk, a huge armoire, and a comfortable easy chair. I remembered how Eleanora had been in ecstasies over the stateroom she occupied on that Caribbean cruise. But I didn't want to think about that during the hours I spent alone in my stateroom—I wanted to let my thoughts dwell on the problem that had been uppermost in my mind for the better part of a year, that of your future, my dear child.

I blame myself in part for what happened. I should have found some way of buying off Delcannon and Ormley before things went too far, but I was foolish enough to think that Eleanora would come to her senses and see them for the spongers and charlatans they were. That, however, was not to be; from the time Lenore married Scale—a most successful marriage—Eleanora had her heart set on seeing you established with a coronet and a castle, and when Delcannon and Ormley appeared on the scene, she wasted no time in spreading her net. Unfortunately, I was powerless to stop her; she held, as they say (and so I thought at the time) all the trumps, and I was in a poor position to move against her wishes.

Two separate events militated against me: first, shortly after Alicia was born, Eleanora's father, Samuel van Alstyne, died and left his entire estate (valued at approximately fifty million) to her, his only child. I myself am worth between twenty and twenty-five million, but that inheritance of hers marks the turning point in our relationship, the point at which she obtained the upper hand, a position which was strengthened considerably by what happened later.

After Lenore's birth, Eleanora informed me that not only were there to be no more children, but also that she no longer desired my presence in her bedchamber. The birth had been a difficult one, and for a time I thought that her reaction was only temporary, that she would, after a reasonable time, welcome me back to her. Such was not the case; as far as Eleanora was concerned, all conjugal activity was a thing of the past, with the result that it wasn't long before I found ways of pleasing myself.

We lived in apparent harmony, surface harmony, I should say, until 1893, when Eleanora's hold over me became even firmer. Let me say in all honesty that I do not know whether you are my child or not, Maida; I shall never know for certain (although you have my deep-blue eyes), but that in no way lessens my affection for you. I hold you more dear than any of my other children, although Jerome has always delighted me, and I sincerely admire Peter's independence of mind.

This is what happened: A young woman with whom I had been intimate, and whom I knew only as Marguerite, died after giving birth to a child. Her sister, a woman of the same calling, brought the infant to my house on the night of January 31, 1893. Fortunately I answered the ring of the doorbell myself, having told the butler I intended to sit up for a while, and that he needn't wait to turn out the lights.

Before I could stop her, the woman thrust the infant into my arms, at the same time saying that for a certain sum of money she would refrain from publicizing the fact that I was the father. I argued that she couldn't possibly have any proof of my paternity, that I knew there had been other men who visited Marguerite (I even knew who some of them were), and that she'd better take the child and leave. At that moment Eleanora came down the stairs.

I should explain here that one thing, probably the only thing, that my wife feared in this world was scandal. Her position in society, solid and seemingly impregnable, took precedence over all else, and she guarded it with her life. She knew only too well how easily she could be toppled from her little throne by even the slightest deviation from the established norms of propriety. Any hint of illegitimacy would mean instant, absolute ostracism. If you understand this, you will see why she took the steps I shall describe.

The woman, who gave her name as Nell Currie, repeated her story to Eleanora, and from that moment my wife took charge of the situation. In less than a quarter of an hour she had paid the woman with bills from the small wall safe in her bedroom, extracted a written promise of silence from her, and sent her on her way. She closed the outer door firmly on our uninvited guest, and only then did she look directly at me as I stood holding you.

"Eleanora, there's no proof ..." I began.

"Perhaps not, Julian," she said quietly, "but there is certainly doubt, and you know the saying about where there is smoke ... Now, let me think what to do."

"I don't suppose—"

"Be quiet, Julian. I am trying to think. We can't take her to an orphanage because we might be seen. Any number of people are apt to be still abroad. We'd be on our way home from the opera right now ourselves if Eulalia hadn't begged me for my box for tonight. And I happen to know that the Foresters, two doors away from us, are entertaining at a midnight supper tonight. No, we can't run the risk of being seen, not when everyone knows we did not attend the opera tonight."

"Well then, what are we to do? We can't put the helpless infant out on the street."

"There is just one thing to be done, Julian, and we shall do it. We will keep this child as one of our own, and incidentally, as a constant reminder of your folly."

"But how will you explain—"

"You will leave that to me, as you will leave everything else that concerns this family to me from now on."

I knew I had no choice.

The following morning she had her story ready. She announced to the staff that shortly before she died, a recently widowed cousin of hers had requested her doctor to take the baby to us, certain that we would give the infant a home.

"I have arranged for a nurse to take charge of her," she said, looking at the group assembled in the dining room, "and I will expect all of you to cooperate with her. The baby's name is Maida, Maida Jardine, and she will grow up with the rest of my children."

They swallowed the story whole, and there were even murmurs of what a wonderful thing she was doing for the poor little motherless babe. To Alicia and Lenore, who were only four and three at the time, she merely said that they had a new baby sister; they were too young to know anything about pregnancy or childbirth. Fortunately, the three boys were away at school, and when they came home for the Easter vacation, they seemed not at all surprised that their mother had produced another offspring. As an added precaution, Eleanora replaced the staff, one by one. I think that's when Collins came.

What about her women friends? Wouldn't they have been aware of Eleanora's condition? Not necessarily. You see, she had been under the weather, some kind of grippe or other, since Christmas, and before that we had been in Europe for two months, seeing the sights in Rome and Vienna and spending money in Paris. Also, while Eleanora has dozens of female acquaintances, women she sees at stated and generally formal occasions, I have never known her to have any close friends, ones with whom she would be apt to exchange confidences. She has always been more interested in private conversations with men. Besides that, at the time of your arrival, pregnancy was still a hushed-up topic among the Brahmins, and the coutouriers patronized by women of fashion were adept at producing gowns designed to conceal the inevitable changes in the female figure.

Well, Eleanora not only carried out her ruse successfully, but she also reinforced her hold over me, a hold she could tighten at will. I did not know how much longer I could stand it, but I knew this: whether you are my daughter or not, I would do everything in my power to see you happily married to the man of your choice. This is the only path that will lead to peace of mind for me, and one that may earn me redemption of a sort.

Those were some of the thoughts that occupied me during my leisure hours aboard the *Sequoia,* and by the time we docked at Southampton, a plan of action had begun to take shape in my mind. We entrained for London at once, where Rellenbach immediately went into conference with his British partners to complete some large, no doubt profitable, financial venture. He left the rest of us to our own devices, for which I was grateful, as it enabled me to start on an investigation of the house of Delcannon.

It did not take me long to locate the estate of the earl on the outskirts of the village of Mereton in Hertfordshire. A somewhat dilapidated stone wall, overhung with trees and shrubs that needed pruning, fronted the property, and no one prevented me from pushing open the rusted iron bars of the gate next to a small building I took to be the keeper's lodge. After instructing my driver to wait, I left the car and walked slowly down a curving, tree-lined drive, and just as the house itself came into view, I caught sight of a workman approaching me.

When I said I was a friend of the earl, and that I was hoping to find him in residence, the fellow laughed before introducing himself as Tom Geddes, the caretaker.

"You'll not find him here, sir," he said ruefully. "Seldom it is that he spends any time here. Off to the high society spots he is. Spends most of the time in London, when he's not in foreign parts, that is. A shame, sir, the way he's let this place go. Falling apart it is, not like in the old days. Look there."

I turned in the direction in which he pointed and we walked on until we stood a hundred yards or so away from a house in the same state of disrepair as the wall and the grounds. In spite of the peeling paint, the boarded-up windows, and the chipped stonework of the terrace, however, the building had a certain dignity, and a definite appeal, with the pure lines of its Georgian architecture unspoiled by later additions, Victorian or otherwise. I felt strongly attracted to it, and as I examined the stone facade glowing in the light of the late-afternoon sun, I pictured the high-ceilinged, perfectly proportioned rooms, an interior meant for repose and pleasure, not for showy display like the mansions so dear to Eleanora's heart.

Tom Geddes, obviously glad to have company, talked freely about his lot and about his employer as we made our way down the drive to my car, and on the way back to London I reviewed in my mind what I had learned from him. The countess, Viscount

Ormley's mother, died in 1907, and after her death the place rapidly went downhill. It was she, according to my informant, who had kept the earl and her son in line. Apparently she'd been renowned for her beauty, and also blessed with a head for business, and had managed to keep the place going with such funds as the estate possessed.

"Don't know what they did with the money after she went," the caretaker said, shaking his head in perplexity. "Spent it down to the last shilling, no doubt. Sold off all the livestock, let the farm go, a bloody shame, that's what. We heard of them going off to the Riviera, Paris, and the like, and now it's America, but what they're after in all them foreign parts when there's things to be done here—well, it's none of my business, but hard to understand it is."

I know only too well what Delcannon and Ormley are after in America, I thought grimly, vowing silently that they would not get it through marriage with you. I turned back for a last look at the once lovely house before it was obscured by the dense foliage of the low-hanging branches on either side of the drive, and after thanking Geddes for his time, made my way back to London.

Rellenbach had planned a Mediterranean cruise for us, with stopovers along the Riviera and then on to Greece before sailing for New York.

"Ah, Crete!" I heard him exclaim. "Age-old Crete, famed in song and story, home of the minotaur! A wonderful place to relax in, far away from the cares of the office. I'm thinking of buying a place there."

Even if I had not been deeply concerned about you, I would not have looked with favor upon the prospect of four or five more weeks of enforced idleness aboard the yacht. I'd had enough of that.

At the first opportunity I cabled instructions to Jack Mintz, my confidential assistant, and waited as patiently as I could for his reply. It couldn't have arrived at a more opportune moment. Two nights before we were to leave on the cruise we were having dinner in Rellenbach's suite at Claridge's, and our host was in a particularly cheerful mood. We had reached the brandy-and-cigar stage when Mintz's cable concerning an emergency that required my immediate presence was handed to me. Rellenbach blustered a bit about the incompetence of subordinates, but when I mentioned the vast sum involved in the transaction, he agreed that I had no choice but to return to New York. Actually a similar matter on a considerably smaller scale had been pending when we sailed, and I knew that if Rellenbach were to bring up the subject in the future, I could cover myself.

"We'll miss you, Julian," he said the next day as I was taking my leave, "but our loss is the lovely Eleanora's gain. Fortunate, isn't it, that you were able to book passage on the *Mauretania?*"

It occurred to me then, and not for the first time, that if I were out of the way it would not be long before "the lovely Eleanora" and her millions belonged to Richard Rellenbach. His own wife, the former Regina Kent, had died five or six years ago. He had all the money he could possibly want; maybe he was just lonesome. With that thought I dismissed the great financier from my mind and devoted myself to the problem of finding and protecting you, Maida.

By the time we docked in New York, after a tiresome but uneventful crossing, I had decided that the first thing to do would be to hire a private detective, no matter what the cost, and no matter how much Eleanora protested. After covering up the story of your birth, my wife could not, I reasoned, expose my indiscretion without leaving herself open to society's criticism. Why hadn't I thought of that years ago? How could I, an astute and successful man of affairs, have been so stupid? Was I afraid of losing her? It would have made all the difference in our lives had I pointed that out to her, but I hadn't. Yes, I'd been afraid of losing her then, but no longer. Circe is dead.

With that in mind I made my way to the train and arrived at the house in Glen Cove shortly after four o'clock in the afternoon.

Tired, hot, and somewhat out of sorts, I let myself into the house, wanting nothing so much as a cool bath and a nap before dinner, neither of which I was to have. A quick glance around the drawing room as I made my unannounced entrance made my heart sink, ill prepared as I was for an immediate confrontation.

Let me see if I can put it down clearly so that you will not be as confused as I was at the time: My mind had barely registered the fact that my wife, looking unusually pale and tired, was entertaining Delcannon and Ormley before you, my darling, hurled yourself into my arms. You were crying in short, painful gasps, like a helpless, wounded creature. I was patting you gently on the back as you clung to me—I don't remember anyone ever clinging to me before—when Gus Schilling and Oliver were announced and there was all the brouhaha about a Miss Wick and a lost earring.

When that had all been explained, Eleanora took me aside to bring up the subject of your marriage, but I cut her short.

"That will do, Eleanora," I said firmly. "You will leave this to me, and you will do as I say unless you want to be involved in the scandal of the decade—perhaps of the century."

Shocked by my rebellion against her authority, she stood still for a moment or two, hands clenched and eyes blazing, as I turned to greet Delcannon and Ormley as civilly as I could.

In order to forestall any discussion concerning future plans for you, I announced (but quietly) that I would confer with them in my study the following morning. Eleanora sighed and within a few minutes left to change for dinner.

I believe the meal that night would have been eaten in complete silence had it not been for the account Gus gave us (with your help) of his search for the Czarina's ruby, a typical Schilling caper if I ever heard one.

The earl and his son retired to their rooms in the guest suite immediately after dinner, and after making sure that Gus had everything he needed, I left him in Oliver's capable hands and started for my own room. I had not hesitated to invite them to spend the night, knowing as I did that Eleanora always had rooms ready for the unexpected guest. I must give her credit for that.

On my way to my own quarters I was surprised to see a young man half-asleep in an armchair in the alcove opposite your door.

"Mrs. Jardine's orders, sir," he said in reply to my question regarding his presence. "I am to see that Miss Maida does not leave the premises."

"Well, you'll follow my orders now. Stay here for the night, and make sure no one *enters* my daughter's room, and report to *me* first thing in the morning. Is that clear?"

"Yes, sir, perfectly clear," he replied, looking somewhat puzzled. As well he might, I thought.

I had begun to undress, just taken off my jacket, when Eleanora knocked on my door. She wanted to talk to me, she said.

"Tomorrow, Eleanora," I said as she came into the room, the long skirt of her dinner dress making the familiar swishing sound as she crossed the carpet. "I'm dead tired."

"This will only take a few minutes. I must say, Julian, that I am appalled at your behavior."

"And I by yours, my dear."

"Who is this man, Schilling, anyway? And why is he staying here?"

"He is an old friend of mine, and one of the wealthiest men in New York, Eleanora; he is staying here because I invited him. Now please go, and let me get to bed."

"I have not finished, Julian. I want to make it clear to you that the only possible thing for Maida to do is to marry the viscount."

"I will never permit that."

"Can you not see that she must? After disfiguring him so badly, she has no choice. She is obligated—she has completely ruined his life."

"I refuse to discuss this nonsense tonight. Go to bed, Eleanora. You look pale; have you been ill? You'd better get some rest. I will see you with the others in my study at ten o'clock tomorrow morning." With that I took her firmly by the arm and escorted her to the door, wishing I could put her out of my life as easily as I put her out of my room.

The next morning, as you will remember, I made short shrift of the earl and his son with a firm rejection of Ormley's proposal, and then arranged for you to live with Jerome and Maria, at least for the time being. For the next several weeks Eleanora and I maintained what, for want of a more original phrase, I shall call "an armed truce."

That came to an end when the news broke that Delcannon and Ormley were bringing suit against us. Eleanora took to her bed, refusing to see anyone for two days. On the evening of the third day, when I arrived home from a dinner at Jerome's, I found her in the drawing room, talking animatedly to Richard Rellenbach as they planned a cruise down the coast of South America on the *Sequoia*. She left at the end of the week, saying she wasn't sure when she would return. Her departure was a great relief to me, and left me free to devote myself to you and your troubles.

A more nerve-racking fortnight than the one that followed the opening of the trial I have never experienced. I could not tell from one day to the next whether it would be necessary for me to reveal the part I had played in the wounding of the viscount or not. Now that it is all over, however, I feel that I must make it known, if only to you. A coward's way out? Probably, but so be it.

When I heard the noise in the kitchen the night of February 15, 1911, I thought that you, in your hurried flight, had stumbled over a chair or something else in the dim light. After a moment or two, when there was no further sound, I went quietly down the back stairs to make sure you had gotten away safely, and there I found Ormley, sprawled out on the kitchen floor.

Until he confessed at the trial that Eleanora had arranged for him to stay overnight, I had no idea why the fellow was in my house. She must have slipped downstairs after I went to my room and let him in. What a conniving woman! She would stop at nothing to get you married to a titled Englishman! Nothing!

When I saw Ormley lying on the floor, my floor, I was suddenly so enraged at the duplicity of the man that I wanted to kill him, then and there. Although he was bleeding from the side of his head, he was still breathing, and without hesitation I pulled a knife from the rack over the chopping board, intending to finish him off. I went so far as to cut a gash in his forehead before I came to my senses. I could not, even in my rage, commit murder in cold blood.

I washed and dried the knife and returned it to its holder. Just in time, too, for moments later Collins came into the kitchen and found me staring down at the unconscious figure on the floor.

I pretended to be as nonplussed as he was, and suggested that Ormley had surprised an intruder and had been overpowered by him. Collins agreed with me, and the fact that the back door, the one the tradesmen use, was partly open supported my theory.

It was never necessary for me to admit all this at the trial, thank God, but there is no getting away from the truth: I wanted to kill a man, and almost did. Maida, my Maida, with my own dark-blue eyes and so many of my values and characteristics, you were worth saving from that charlatan at any cost.

You will be dismayed, my darling, even shocked when you read this, but I feel happier now, knowing that someday *you* will know the whole truth. Believe me.

Julian Jardine

chapter twenty-one

I *was* dismayed and shocked the first time I read my father's letter, and for some weeks I mentioned it to no one. I needed time to accept that I had been born an illegitimate child, and was not even legally adopted like Christina. I despaired at the thought of being the child of a prostitute and a man who thought nothing of having extramarital relations. But as the weeks and months went by, my attitude changed from one of resentment to one of acceptance, even gratitude.

In many rereadings of my father's letter—and I am convinced he *was* my father—I came to realize how much I must have meant to him for him to submit for so long to the sometimes outrageous demands of his wife. (I can no longer say "my mother.") He put up with a great deal from her; her narrow view of life and her deference to society's rules must have nearly driven him mad at times. It is ironic, in a way, that because of her overriding fear of scandal in the society she worshiped, I escaped the orphanage and possibly an orphan train.

Three months elapsed before I finally showed the letter to Mark and Jerome, both of whom agreed that after the shock of being presented with a newborn infant, Father had acted only in my best interests. They were also adamant in their belief that there could be no doubt that I was his daughter.

"You certainly do have his eyes, Maida," Jerome said, "and your left eyebrow has the same little quirk in it that his had."

"His Marguerite must have been a lovely woman," Mark said, putting his arm around me, "to have produced you."

"I'm sure she was," Jerome agreed, "and I am equally sure we all would have loved her."

"I like to think they had some happy times together," I said. "I don't think he had too many such times with Mother—I should say with Mrs. Jardine. But Mark, how do you feel now? First you knew me as Mary Wick on the roof of a burning building, next you knew me as Maida Jardine in a court case, and now as—"

"How many times do I have to tell you that it's *you* I love, no matter what your name or your ancestry?" he expostulated before kissing me as fervently as he did the night he asked me to marry him.

"He means it, little sister," Jerome said, glancing at his watch. "Believe me, he means it."

Mark did mean it, and we've had the kind of marriage Father had wanted for me. I think of Father often, and yesterday, when I went to the city, he was very much on my mind. I wanted to see the Jardine mansion one more time before it disappeared forever, taking with it memories of a way of life that has almost been forgotten. As I stood on the opposite side of Sixty-first Street, looking up at the library on the second floor, I pictured Father sitting there in his oversized leather armchair, and for a moment I thought I saw a wisp of smoke from his cigar curling up against the glass of the window.

I had cut out the photograph of the house from the *Times*, and when I arrived home from the city that day I clipped it to Father's letter. Somehow it seemed appropriate, even though the windows of the library do not show up too well in the picture.